A PERILOUS LIFE

BY

Lociano Benjamin

By Lociano Benjamin

Tears of Love (2002), Pensée Universelle,
Paris, France

*500 Years of Exploitation: A Study of Diplomacy
and Economics in Haiti* (2010), Tate
Publishing, Mustang, Oklahoma

Title: A Perilous Life
Author: Lociano Benjamin
Editing: Kate Keverline and Joe E. Sully
Layout and Cover: Kate Keverline

Bridgevision Production LLC
PO BOX 9767
Washington, DC 20016
erilandesully@gmail.com
www.bridgevisionllc.com

Library of Congress Catalogue-in-Publication Data is available upon request. Originally published: 2021.
ISBN: 978-1-7376789-0-8

PROLOGUE

Qué es la vida? Una ilusión
Qué es la vida? Un frenesí
Porque la vida es un sueño
Y los sueños, sueños son
> *- La vida es un Sueño*, Calderón de la Barca

Who am I? In the delusion and frenzy of life, feeling helpless, I want to sink—to bury myself on this white beach with warm sand, still, at this hour of dusk. Some would envy me, seeing me lean against a convertible car in my white linen suit, my eyes lost on the glowing horizon of this Caribbean coast, but I know better.

A grain of sand, a microscopic particle in the midst of thousands, millions, billions of a kind, join together, stretched so beautifully along the beaches where the tourists dream. The lovers lie down there to kiss each other, and let themselves be caught in the glamor of romanticism. The children build castles dedicated to destruction, an ephemeral dream. The fishermen go there to scrutinize the waves and assess their chances of earning their daily bread.

The sand of the dunes in flamboyant colors creates mirages in the deserts, which mislead the most daring or the most unlucky. This golden dust can be reduced to nothing, remodeled indefinitely by the whims of the storms; alas, nature often reminds us of order, it is the only master.

White sand, golden sand
Red sand, black sand
Sand of life and sand of death
Sand of my despair.
Where I am buried without fighting
And your memory, your memories
O fickle and worshiped women
Risen like a tornado of sand.
Should I survive or give up my soul.
                                   - *Dunes*, M.H.

MY MOTHER'S LOVE

Antan D'avant

...Petit-Poucet dreamer, I was in my race
Rhymes. My hostel was at the Big Dipper
My stars in the sky had a sweet rustle.

And I listened to them sitting by the roadside.
Those good nights of September when I felt Dewdrops
Like a wine of vigor.

Where, rhyming in the midst of fantastic shadows
Like lyres, I pulled the elastics
Of my injured shoes, One foot near my
heart

- Bohemia, Arthur Rimbaud

7

In the neighborhood of Martissant 7 where I was born, we all knew each other. Children laughed and played as we filled the streets of our happy din. My three younger brothers and I made a good fuss, and we fell to our skinned knees more often than not. However, I already distinguished myself by a dreamier and more naive side.

Ever since I knew how to read, all my attention went to reading poetry, whose rhymes, special order of words, and powerful images filled me with overwhelming emotion. I spent a lot of time writing poems dedicated to nature, angels, stars, and my mother on notebooks or any paper I could find.

She smiled with all the tenderness of the world and said to me, "OK, you will be a poet one day, my Benjie, but for now, go get me my commissions. I must prepare food."

During the day, my mother, Marguerite, first started the fire, prepared our clothes, and as soon as we had lunch and were ready to go to school, she set out on her own to accomplish her grueling tasks among the bourgeois of the beautiful neighborhoods. She worked tirelessly and was honest and punctual. For that, she was appreciated by all her employers. She applied a strict education, according to the principles of my father and our church, but always with kindness and patience. She scolded when us kids quarreled, asking us to think about our brothers' love and forgiveness. She spoke to us about tolerance and fraternity. "Love one another," she often said, shaking her head. We knew that compassion and family were values we had to respect.

I became aware very early of her tiredness. She came home in the evenings, and then went back to work. We were punished if we did not do our homework seriously and silently. For her, cleaning, washing our clothes, and preparing meals is what she took care of extremely well. We studied vigilantly under the lamp of the dining room awaiting the return of my father, exhausted too. He questioned us about our lessons as soon as he had freshened up, donned an immaculate bathing suit and wide trousers, and presided over the dinner of peas, rice, fried chicken, or fish we were having. In a warm family atmosphere, we each told the events of the day. These evening meals were an opportunity for my father to teach us rules of life and to develop our curiosity with anecdotes about his many travels and knowledge of other countries. To us, these seemed like fantastic tales.

Although I was able to attend school at the Franco-Haitian Adventist Institute, a private institute, we were not very rich. My mother's long hours of work were only for our education and clothes so that we could be placed among the elites of the city. I felt all the more indebted to my mother because some of our neighbors took their children out of school at the age of thirteen or fourteen to support the family by doing odd jobs. Striving to be the first in the class to justify these sacrifices, I went to sleep every night dreaming of the day when I would see my mother in a beautiful floral dress, white hat, and necklace of gold balls at church, taking my father's arm. He would be dressed in his light suits, which he wore so well. I saw them joining a pavilion nestled in the greenery on the heights of Port-au-Prince in a convertible American car that I would have bought them. They would live without a care, with a young and devoted servant to relieve my poor mother of all her duties.

I imagined them seated at a café on boulevard Jean Jacques Dessalines, greeted by all Port-au-Prince, who murmured, "See, these are the parents of the diplomat and ambassador to the UN. You know, I knew them when they lived humbly in Martissant."

Pride would illuminate my mother's beautiful face and put a satisfied little smile on my father's lips. I gave myself the lead in a future whose distance I could not measure.

My parents were a nice couple, despite their difference in age. From his long stay abroad in Cuba, my father had a taste for discovery, a rich culture, a philosophy of righteousness, and the gift of social climbing (by the sweat of his brow and on his own merits). He spoke several languages fluently, including Spanish, English, and French, and always encouraged us to master the science of languages to better communicate with other people of the Caribbean. My ambitions took on another dimension, and I promised to conquer America and even Europe.

If my parents spoke to us or talked in Creole, it was appropriate to communicate in French at home, in the interest of our social rise. Our modest income certainly made us privileged children of the district, but never were we hungry. Once or twice a year, we went with the family to buy clothes. On the sidewalks of Port-au-Prince sprawled all merchandise *pèpè*: T-shirts, jeans of all colors, sneakers, sports bags, all kinds of belts, ties, shirts, skirts, and blouses. What seemed to me like prestigious American companies were in fact only scrap, unsold, or second-hand products straight from the United States.

This giant neighbor exalted me as much as France, and I was convinced that my destiny would take me there one day. On Sunday's, when my parents thought they could spare some gourdes from our budget, it was like a feast day. My father tried his luck at the "lottery" to try to multiply his modest stake, and we were entitled to an ice cream. Leisurely strolling on the opulent avenues of the city center, we looked at the shop windows, enjoying the colorful spectacle of the busy crowd. On the terraces of the cafés, musicians performed, and some couples writhed to the rhythm of swaying waltzes. This show delighted us, and from that time, I kept the taste of dance in the rhythm of our countries. In the evening, our little family returned home. Happy with the purchases made and the sweet taste of ice cream and treats still on our lips, my brothers and I danced home under the tender eye of our parents.

At seven o'clock, chocolate was served on the table, and our cups were filled with a tasty beverage that smoked in the white enamel pan. The horn of the baker's van was heard at the corner of the street, and the agitation made the neighboring houses shudder. The housewives, wearing flowery blouses with hair curlers on their heads, and children like me, washed and clean to go to school, crowded into a joyous cacophony around the van. Hand tightened on the two gourdes that mommy entrusted to me, I took my place politely in the queue.

"Fifty cents of brioche, please!"

I was very tall for my twelve years of age. I had not yet acquired the confidence of adolescents, but the respect I was taught in regard to adults made me patiently wait my turn. The old Domitian complained for five minutes of her rheumatism, and the beautiful Heloise spent three minutes exchanging glances and some jesting pleasantries with Jacob the baker, a notorious womanizer. We all knew that Jacob was her lover, and evil tongues said that he was already married and had children in another city. However, Heloise did not do anything about it and acted shamelessly with him in public.

They gave me the ball of sweet bread that would be our breakfast, with a big smile, "So, Benjie, still determined to become our future diplomat or the *Césaire* of Haiti?"

Laughs erupted, but they were kind. I knew my family was well respected in the neighborhood for our kindness, our good education, and our honorability.

In two minutes, the milk truck and the grocer will point their colorful hoods around the corner. I knew I had to wait to complete the commissions that Mom asked me to do for her.

"Fifty cents of milk, please. Fifty cents of sugar, please."

I hugged these basic foods that will lead to the first family meal of the day, aware that so many other families could not even afford this minimum of food. Every day, I blessed my parents for their dedication to our well-being. I blessed the Lord who provided for our table every day and allowed us to study to get out of our living condition—to climb the social ladder and help our poorest brothers to our tower. The smell of the hot and supple brioche made my mouth water. I remembered that I was hungry and that my little brothers were waiting for me to break the fast of the night.

THE POET WITH THE BROKEN HEART

A few years later, after my father had the opportunity to start a business and open his own bakery, our situation became more comfortable. We moved to a lighter and more spacious house in Bizoton in the eighties.

I chose a path of professional training to perform faster. I knew, nevertheless, that I would pursue studies one day that would lead me much further and would be more in line with my natural inclinations: writing, belles-lettres, languages, and diplomacy. My ambitions had no limit, but I told myself that everything came in its time.

I attended the Canadian-Haitian College, obtaining my professional baccalaureate and my graduation diploma. I met endearing men and women with extraordinary charisma. These people constantly supported me and urged me to persevere, including my friend Frantz Berrouet. My gratitude for them remains unshakable. We were the first generation of romance.

When I was eighteen years old, I set my heart on a girl who attended a nearby college, whose parents went to the same church as us on Sunday's. They greeted my family, but did not really know us.

Noéliane became my muse. She inspired me with inflamed verses that I dedicated to her in my heart, unable to reveal anything to her. I met her on the way to school and gave her furtive glances. She passed without seeing me, accompanied by a friend named Clarisse, who all the boys at school said was not shy and rather sassy. Some boys boasted either of having kissed her or gone further into more intimate relations, even insinuating that Noéliane was beginning to follow the same path.

These remarks annoyed me. I sometimes defended the girls, but I dared not compromise too much for fear that others would find out I was plagued by the thought of Noéliane and decide to tell her things about me. I loved her and respected her. The remarks made against Clarisse also made her upset, and I could not accept that.

I daydreamed, sitting in front of the kitchen door with my chin in my clasped hands and elbows on my knees. The little book of poetry I just started fell to the ground, but I did not want to pick it up. In front of my half-closed eyes was the figure of Noéliane, supple and thin as the vine whose name she bore. I dreamt of her curves, her thin waist, and her soft neck. I remembered her sweet smile and gaze like calm water. Her skin was a tinted color of milk caramel with baby dimples on her cheeks. I found her so stunning.

My mother observed me without saying anything. She made me understand, while preparing a coconut flan for dessert, that she knew my secret.

"Hey, man, wap mouri pour ti fi saa, fok ou wé kle nan kè ou wi, si ou vlé pale avèl, pa reté tan ké vè ya vine nan fri ya, paske zanmi saa pa bon pou li ditou," which meant, "My poor boy, you are dying of love for this girl, you must have a clear heart."

"If you want to speak to her," she said to me, "Do not wait for too long because I do not think her friend is a good example for her, and it's better that things are clear between you two."

I remained perplexed because I never imagined I would be discovered. "Mother, mother, how did you know?"

"I know my children," she told me. "For weeks you have written at least three notebooks of poetry, especially on Sunday after mass, or when you come home from school. You always sit with your eyes fixed on the young lady. But I can tell you that she, too, has been looking at you for a few Sunday's, even if she is doing her *mijaurée*. I admit that she is a very beautiful girl, but I know how she is inside. That is also important, my boy, so remember that."

I never doubted Mom's judgment, and that day her clairvoyance amazed me and made me happy. She was truly an exceptional person. She had an intelligent heart.

I decided to get closer to my beautiful and ask her to go out with me. I had virtually no relationship experience other than two or three furtive kisses, stolen from a school dance the previous year, from a classmate who had more experience. She mocked my clumsiness when I put my lips on hers. She gave me some "real" kisses like grown-ups, as she said. She let me caress her body, through her dress first, then more intimate places. (Under the condition that I only use my hands and that I buy her a drink and a slice of cake at the movies.) I saved the five gourdes my mother gave me every Sunday, so I had some money reserved. I promised her everything she wanted if she allowed me to go further. This is how I discovered the hidden mysteries of the female being.

I recalled foggy, elusive visions when I took the dark alley home and saw our neighbor Heloise leaning against a wall with Jacob the baker standing between her legs. Making myself discreet, almost invisible, I heard them breathe very loudly as they emitted a groan and panted while Heloise adjusted her skirts and Jacob pulled up his pants. Then, they kissed for a long time on the lips. I spied on them, trying to imagine exactly what they were doing. These thoughts provoked me with funny desires. I felt new emotions and I breathed, panting like them. I knew that I should not have seen such things, but I did not run behind a wall feeling embarrassed. I tried to see more, cheeks on fire. This was how adults made love, and I envied them to have this magical power to find the one who spontaneously responded to their desire. The few nocturnal pollutions I had as a teenager agitated me and left me panting and shameful when I discovered my bed in the morning. I can certainly say now that the desire and kisses opened guilty but pleasant horizons.

This memory made me think that I had become a real male, so I thought that, when the time came, I would impress my sweet friend and that we would feel these extreme emotions together. From that day, I multiplied the opportunities of meeting and greeting, and I invited her to get an ice cream or fruit juice in a cafeteria frequented by people our age. I made myself her knight, but I never dared to reveal to her my true feelings. It seemed to me that she heard and shared them. I wrote her poems burning with love, and she listened pensively without saying anything. Sometimes she nodded and a put her hand on mine, which was wonderful. I wished every day for the moment when I could press her against me and give her the languorous kiss I imagined, like in the movies. For the moment, we discussed ideas, shared laughter, exchanged jokes, and talked about our career goals.

Noéliane wanted to become a teacher or a nurse, professions that our country really needed. I appreciated her vocation for children and the sick, but I couldn't stop thinking of a more physical relationship. The thought obsessed me as she spoke, and I stared eagerly at her bulging lips. I was convinced not to go far with her, as with my classmate a few months prior, so as not to frighten her. She seemed pure and innocent.

On Sunday's, I took the liberty of sitting near her under the benevolent eyes of our parents. They were more familiar with each other because my mother, under the pretext of preparing the parish feast, invited them to coffee one afternoon. They feasted on piles of diligently made cookies, donuts, and pies. In turn, we were invited to the parents' home of "my friend" because her mother wanted to compete in generosity and acknowledge mine.

However, our love was still at the same stage. I feared scaring her and ruining something by passing more intimate gestures. My desire tortured me and became more and more apparent. I was troubled and uncomfortable in front of her. I had to take courage into my own hands and tell her how much I loved her. I feared seeing her less often because the holidays were approaching, so I had to decide. How do I find an opportunity to spend several hours with her and reach my goals?

I did not want Clarisse, who followed her like a shadow, to accompany us. I decided to talk to Benny, a school friend who often spoke to Clarisse and seemed to know her well.

"Clarisse? Do you want me to invite Clarisse to see Noéliane?" Benny burst out laughing when I told him of my intentions. "Are you serious? You know that Clarisse I know her from every angle, he laughed again, it will not be a surprise to me to do it once more ... Are you paying for the tour? We should go all four, so you will lose your virginity!"

Was he was making fun of me? His vulgarity and lack of respect left me stunned and angry, but I needed him. I pretended not to understand, and we agreed to go to a club frequented by young people from a different neighborhood to avoid attracting attention and seeing the two girls from the previous Saturday.

I reviewed the shirts that my mother had on a hanger and the two ties I wore on Sunday's or holidays, but none seemed good enough for the night of my "pseudo-engagement." I did not know how much my mother could have invested in new clothes for this occasion because even though our situation had improved comfortably, studies were getting more and more expensive. My brothers were growing up, and my dad had started his business. A little disillusioned at the sight of the collars and cuffs a little used and the color of my ties too dark, which I judged suddenly old-fashioned, I looked sadly at my wardrobe.

As always, in the nature of my mother, the good fairy came into my room. Seeing my disappointed look and the shirts spread on the bed, she understood. With her kind smile and soft voice, she said to me, "So, my boy, what's the problem?"

I was on the verge of tears. "How do I confess my love to Noéliane on the dance floor without nice clothes?"

Mom took me in her arms and whispered, "Do not worry, we will fix it. Can you wait until tomorrow?"

"Of course, Mom, it is for Saturday," I replied, biting my tongue too late because I had revealed some of the secret.

My mother smiled again. "Ah, Benjie, you will always be as innocent as an angel. I will take care of that, my son, but you have to worry about

23

something else, too. I know what youth are passionate about. Do not commit the irreparable, and always respect the girl you love. I am going to see your father. You have to talk to him, man to man, because he will understand these things."

"Thanks, mom, I love you so much."

My mother's eyes were suddenly wet, and she turned away. "You grow so fast, my good man, so fast."

The same evening, my father went out on the doorstep to light his evening pipe and sit in his wicker chair. A small glass of rum in his hand, he settled there and asked me to keep him company. His request alarmed me at first, but with his habitual calmness and his learned air, he told me the ways of love.

He handed me two condoms that I dared not touch, asking me to use them. This idea never occurred to me, despite the science courses we had taken on STDs and contraception. Like many young teens, when the teachers addressed this chapter, I laughed stupidly with the others. Now this lesson was real, and I was grateful to my father for having this conversation with me.

The next day, when I returned from class, I found on the back of the chair in my room a white shirt with a discreet embroidery and a monogram on the breast pocket, a flowered tie in bright colors, and, resting on the big wooden chest at the foot of my bed, white moccasins with a metal buckle on the side. In my opinion, the most elegant in the world. On my night table was a bottle of *Eau Sauvage* by Christian Dior, which plunged me into perplexity. How could my mother make such expenses? I was stunned, and once again, my gratitude to my parents increased tenfold. Their love of their children amazed me.

Awaiting Saturday, my beating heart counted the hours separating me from the fixed appointment with my friends. The afternoon dragged on, and I boiled with impatience. I took great care getting ready, passing and repassing my reflection in the mirror.

I heard my youngest brother chuckle and say to me, "Are you a minister, or are you going to get married?"

Without saying a word, I did not look up and went quietly out of the house. I discovered with joy the two bank notes that my father or mother had slipped into the pocket of my light jacket. I rushed to the meeting spot. Benny, who looked well groomed, heckled me a little, whistling with admiration when he saw me, "Woah! Good sir. Hi, my prince."

These words made the girls laugh a good deal, and I kissed each of them to continue the joke. Addressing myself to Noéliane, I murmured with love and sincerity in my heart, "Hello, my princess."

She was dressed in white and her curly hair was loose on her shoulders. She smelled like honeysuckle. I saw her for the first time as a young woman and not as the teenage schoolgirl I had known. My savings, plus the generous gesture from my parents, allowed us to take a taxi, which was supreme luxury compared to the dusty tap-tap that would take us to the *Pub de l'Escale*.

We drank several beers, and I tried several times to take Noéliane away, but she looked sad and separated with difficulty from Clarisse. Not denying her reputation, Clarisse kissed Benny full-mouthed, drank cuba libre, a mixture of rum and Coca-Cola that was highly prized by the youth of our generation, and even smoked American cigarettes with gilded ends with a frank and uncomplicated air. Benny took full advantage of it, and sometimes winked at me over the girl's shoulder, holding her close and swaying in an obscene way against her.

Finally, at one point, I was able to kiss my lover, by surprise, and I made this kiss last a very long time. She did not refuse it, and I emboldened, but she was not very cooperative. She never lost sight of the couple that formed Benny and Clarisse. I did not understand this attitude. She let me stroke her hair, face, and waist, but without ardor. Her lack of enthusiasm was obvious, and sooner than expected, she asked me if we could go home because she had enough and felt tired. It was barely ten o'clock.

We took a taxi, and curiously, Clarisse entered the car first, leaning against me, while Benny sat near the driver. Noéliane entered through the other door, sulkily. With no time to react, Clarisse leaned on my shoulder. I tried to stroke Noéliane's hair, passing my arm over Clarisse's head, but in vain. She was not looking for contact. I did not know what to do. We dropped the girls at the foot of their building, and my friend Benny broke away from me and hit me on the shoulder.

"You see, they are all like that: unpredictable," he said. "We must take what we can get. I had fun, my brother."

The end of this evening resonates painfully in me still. My first love had a taste of ashes. In addition, I did not want to ask for explanations because her attitude hurt me. That is why, since that day, I gave myself the label, "The Poet with a Broken Heart."

O sad, sad was my soul
Because of a woman.
I did not comfort myself
Even though my heart was gone.

- *Romances Without Words*, Paul Verlaine

The following gray days, sleepless nights, questions, and sorrows escaped neither my mother nor my family, but they had the tact not to bring it up. Mother Marguerite looked at me sadly, and sometimes a tear shone in her eye, which she wiped discreetly with the end of her white cloth.

I waited for the following Sunday with some perplexity and a lot of anxiety. I wondered if we would repeat this experience. I had to return to class. I walked like a ghost, feeling indifferent, since she had not given me a sign of life since our departure, and I did not meet her on the way to school. Should I go and meet her? Write to her?

One evening, I saw her sitting on a bench where we had spent so many delicious moments. She laughed, bending her head back, and Benny, who was holding her in his arms, covered her delicate neck with kisses. Sitting beside them were Clarisse and William, a boy we knew well, a bad boy who had left school. I understood then. I tried to go unnoticed, despite my height, and took the opposite sidewalk. She was actually in love with Benny. I then remembered her languor, her reverie, her sighs when I read her my love poems. Those only rekindled in her the memory of the one to whom her heart leaned. These emotions were not intended for me. I opened my eyes, feeling the object of her derision, her indifference. My heart was breaking painfully. I certainly felt spite and jealousy, but then I remembered my mother's words: "Respect the girl you love." Should I respect her choice, the ways of her heart, to the detriment of mine? To love is to give without counting. I left without turning around.

You would like to know in words what you have always known in thought. You would always want to touch the naked body of your dreams. It is good that it should be so...

A Perilous Life

The soul does not walk on a ridge, nor does it grow like a reed. It spreads like a lotus with innumerable petals.

- Khalil Gibran

Ruined in my hopes, I did not want to make my mother suffer by showing her my disappointment. The holidays were approaching. Thus, I felt myself open, after tears, to other riches and treasures still unknown. I made the decision to leave and apply for a scholarship to the United States to study, or at least to find a job. I was sad, of course, to leave my parents and my country, but I was convinced that all suffering makes you advance in knowledge and that my destiny forbade resignation. One of my cousins, who lived in New Jersey, often offered for me to join him in his new homeland, swearing that there was room for all hardworking and motivated people like me.

My parents thought this was a wise decision and supported my leaving. "Go, my boy, fulfill your destiny, but do not forget your roots." Marguerite cried secretly, and my brothers had many dreams about the country that was waiting for me. The country where we succeed, where we are rich. They saw this trip as a departure to the "Promised Land" where milk and honey flow. I left my teachers and the old pastor who educated me in the faith, with great emotion. My father hugged me for a long time without saying a word.

THE WEBS OF ARIANE

"I want to live in America."

New York greeted me on a hot August afternoon. My cousin Justin, whom I had not seen since he emigrated, was waiting for me. I found him with joy and accepted his invitation to stay at his home during my stay. The duration of this depended on the job that I would find because, for the moment, I only had a small scholarship for a semester to study English at Brookdale College. Justin had a friend from the Haitian community who ran a small business and seemed interested in my milling and fitter diploma. We met him a few days later.

I took time to discover the city where everything seemed to be rich, abundant, and disproportionate. I admired the beautiful, gleaming cars that ran along the perpendicular avenues. I finally saw the Statue of Liberty, a symbol for us people of slavery, who had shaken the yoke of oppression and created the first black republic. I wandered with Justin on Broadway, dazzled by the bright signs of the shows. I watched the Hudson sink nostalgically in a slight mist one September morning. I looked up, impressed by the Empire State Building and the skyscrapers that bore their name.

Finally, Antonin Mercery agreed to give me a job, which was to change the course of my life. I found a studio in Roselle, and my benefactor cousin helped me move in. Costs were very high, so I took a second job driving for a pizzeria because the late shifts allowed me to work for Antonin during the day, attend English classes three nights a week from 6 p.m. to 8 p.m., and arrive around 9 p.m. at Mario's Place to wash the dishes. I cleaned the cutlery, glasses, and pizza pans with the help of Clara, a very nice and friendly Italian who hummed opera tunes while working. Thanks to her, I discovered *La*

Traviata, Don Juan, Mozart, Donizetti, Puccini, and Verdi.

After hours, Mario allowed us to eat. He would come out with prosciutto, salami, other charcuterie, mozzarella, fresh rosé wine, and a loaf of bread rubbed with garlic, and we would have dinner almost like a family. Clara told me that she wanted to take singing lessons. This small salary at the pizza parlor helped her pay rent to an old aunt who was sheltering her. I confessed that I wanted to be a poet, teacher, and diplomat.

"All of this at the same time?" She nodded doubtfully and murmured, "Poor Benjie, you dream, but it's good to have dreams at your age."

The atmosphere of the pizzeria was warm and good-natured. I worked in a good mood, despite fatigue and lack of sleep. For two years, I settled into a quiet routine interspersed with exams and outings with friends. During the holidays, I traveled to the surrounding states to learn more about this huge country. From time to time, I took a plane to Los Angeles to see Justin's brother, my second cousin, who lived in an incredibly luxurious house. I swore to succeed like him and have a house as beautiful as his with a wonderful woman and two well-behaved children. Their life in California seemed straight out of a TV drama.

I felt lonely, despite a few days and nights spent with women. None of them seemed to be a suitable partner for me. And always, my mind drowned in poetry and literature. I recited Gérard de Nerval, Baudelaire, and Verlaine. My throat was tight, but I could not go back. My destiny was to continue and assimilate as much as possible to my new homeland so that it would become my adopted land forever.

On Sunday's, I went to the Baptist church in my neighborhood and took part in the choir. Singing for the Lord gave me an indescribable exaltation. My progress in English was remarkable, and I spoke fluently, so I decided to continue on to a higher-level course that would allow me to sign up for literature courses and transform my equivalences into French at the university. My ambition gradually grew, took shape.

I gave regular reports to my family in Haiti, and I knew that my parents were really proud of me. Time passed, and so I anchored myself in my new life with pleasure. I thought of my native country, but this separation was a necessary good, an achievement.

I took the steps to obtain American nationality. I was confident and enthusiastic about the future. My university environment helped integrate me without problem in this cosmopolitanism, and I appreciated that more than anything. I loved American society with its quirks and its faults, and I told myself that literature, art, and poetry have no boundaries and are an expression of humanity and universal creative thought. I felt part of a great privileged humanistic movement that opened the way to the world and showed the path of light. I felt great and powerful, deciding to bite into life at the fullest.

I bought my first car, a used Lexus, but it gave me more happiness than a billionaire's Bentley or Rolls. I chose my clothes carefully because I wanted to be elegant, refined, and courteous. What dreams remained to be accomplished! I spent little time comparing my life in Haiti to the one I started in the United States. There was no common measure, no regrets, except that I did not regularly see Mother Marguerite busy cooking and carefully ironing our shirts—smiling, head a little bent to the side, listening to us tell stories. My father swaying in his wicker chair at night, with his old pipe and his little glass of ritual rum. My young, rowdy brothers.

The bustle of Port-au-Prince was nothing compared to the roaring sound of the streets of New York. The street vendors shouted their merchandise, donkeys unloaded their colored baskets at the market, women hailed loudly, and children with bright eyes snuck around barefoot.

Far away, the sound of the sea, the sails of the fishermen, the badly paved streets, and the crowded tap-taps were haunted with, smoke, misery, and sometimes, fear. I closed my eyes and attempted to forget those dark sides of my country... I stored the memories in a drawer of my consciousness.

ARIANE IN MY LIFE

I Believe

I believe that love can last a lifetime
And the heart can define when love is real
I think I can try my luck and say what I feel
I believe in passionate kisses
With tender words that can make
Your clothes fall without violence
All the soft words that I cannot tell you
Explain yourself by looking at you with my eyes.
I think we can be happy
By doing what our hearts say
I believe that love can last a lifetime
And I want to spend this life loving you my love.

- The Tears of Love, Lociano Benjamin

Summer was approaching, and the holidays, too. Knowing that I would have more free time, I decided to take extra work to save money. Antonin knew a taxi driver named Jorge who had to go to Mexico for six weeks to see his family. One day, I heard Jorge complaining about having to leave his usual clientele, so I proposed to take over the devoted route.

Jorge was satisfied, although I could only take this job part-time, especially in the evenings. We made a financial arrangement; and quickly, I found myself in his taxi station that was not very far from my home. I came home very late and missed Mario's last service, but I enjoyed working and gaining experience in different areas, rubbing shoulders with unknown people, while making a better living.

The best part of being a taxi driver: tips. Some Friday or Saturday evenings, I almost doubled the small salary I had agreed with Jorge. When I learned that he was prolonging his stay in Mexico, I agreed to continue to replace him until September. My summer job was assured. Monday was my day-off at Mario's, so I took the taxi more than ten hours in a row.

My weeks were filled. I had no more leisure. I did not know what my fiancée, Ariane, would think because she had lots of free time. She thought about going home to see her family, but the idea of being separated for several days did not really suit us.

"Look, Benjie darling, I do not want to go back to my parents. I should find a job to better afford my next academic year," she said. "There is a problem, however. I have to leave the apartment that I share with my sister because she wants to return home definitively. She has her professional diploma and will be able to find work close to us. I cannot afford the rent alone." She looked really sad.

"So, come live at my place!" I said. My heart was spontaneous.

"Finally!" Ariane cried. "I thought you would never ask me. We can share our love in broad daylight."

She leapt and clapped her hands like the little girl I saw in her. Her joy was really mine, because our weekend meetings, our secret embraces, our always-shortened outings, left me with a taste of sorrow every time I took her home.

I dared to believe in this new, whole happiness. To love and be loved, to share my life with the chosen of my heart, to have a job, to succeed in my studies. It was my dearest wish, and life finally smiled on me. Was I not the happiest man? Had I paved the way for a new, more peaceful, more joyous destiny? If that were the case, I knew that all this was due to meeting "my angel," and I was all the more in love.

We began living together with laughter and kisses. Everything was moved-in in one day. To celebrate, I took the one that, henceforth, I called my wife, to dine with dignity in a Mexican restaurant in honor of Jorge, no doubt, who gave me the opportunity to improve my condition. 548 Main Street, Orange. The place belonged to Jesús Salas, which I heard from Latin American friends.

The entrance to the restaurant *El Bandido* evoked a typical Mexican hacienda. There was even a fake well and a patio with geraniums and potted cacti. As soon as we stepped through the door, we were greeted by a friendly Hispanic waiter who hurried to find us a table. Like all the waiters, he was dressed in a quaint costume of the last century with a wide black belt or red cloth, a white shirt with puffed sleeves, and a black vest.

I was struck by the calculated simplicity of the rustic furniture, sober and cheerful at the same time. The wood tables were oddly painted in bright red, the chairs had high carved backs as in the Spanish style, and the walls were whitewashed — all this was the original condition of the place. I looked with pleasure especially at the paintings, recalling the works of the famous Mexican muralists that tell the history of the Revolution. I thought I recognized scenes from Ribera and Orozco, reproduced by a local artist who was fond of colors with violent contrasts. The characters were reproduced very realistically, and their eyes seemed to search you inside. I was transported out of New Jersey avenues, out of the skyscrapers of New York, from the era of the mobile phone, computer, scientific progress, nuclear programs, and orbital stations in the cosmos.

These *rustauds*, those *peons*, in rags with hollow stomachs, blew the wind of freedom in their country and bled to the four veins by the dictatorship. They freed themselves from it, led by Pancho Villa, the big mustache whose eyes gazed at us from the top of the wall facing our little table. They shed blood for their ideas. I thought of my own story, that of my island. I closed my eyes for a second and saw again Toussaint Louverture's features, his gaze as black as that of Pancho Villa, as if he were staring

42

at me. I had a portrait of him at home. I felt a strange sense of brotherhood for these fighters of the Revolution and shared their avenging ardor, their legitimate claim for the piece of land they cultivated, even though I did not own any home or land and practiced non-violence.

Our human soul is malleable and weak. It can develop addictions in a few minutes. She is strong and invulnerable since she is the breath of God. I smile at myself and at my inner exaltation. Then from dream to reality, there is so much distance. How could I, by this silent evocation, escape the presence of Ariane?

Confused, I came back to reality. Ariane, all beige muslin, took her time sitting on the bench that ran along the wall. She fluffed her hair with an elegant gesture, discreetly pulling her little powder mirror from her bag to check the brilliant pearly pink of her lips. Her chin in her hands and elbows on the table, she now looked attentively at the murals. I felt an irresistible urge to kiss her, to hold her in my arms, but now that we lived under the same roof, I had to master these impulses, since all the time would belong to us from now on.

43

The menu occupied our full attention: *camarones a la Mexicana, nachos con guacamole, quesadillas, tacos, tortillas, chili con carne, parrillada—* we wanted everything. I downed a tequila, then two, then three, offered by the boss, while we started on a strong margarita, then shared a good bottle of very fruity red wine. My companion swallowed a small glass of Licor 43 as a digestive aid after the crème brûlée with orange. I was surprised because she did not drink alcohol in general. Was this day special enough for her to detract from her habits?

Satisfied, and a little gray in my case, I saw life under the best auspices. The coronation of the evening was the serenade given to us by two young *mariachis* who played "La Cucaracha" and "Cielito Lindo," then songs from a more modern repertoire unknown to me, but always in this furious rhythm that translated to the ardor of the Mexican temperament. What an evening! We accompanied the singers for the chorus, clapping our hands to the tempo, and then applauded all at once. Joy and carelessness reigned in this little restaurant.

Con ese lunar, that llevas cielito lindo
Junto has the boca
No lo nadie nadie
Cielito lindo that has even me gusta.

Ay, ay, ay, ay, canta y no llores,
Porque cantando, se alegran,
Cielito lindo
Los corazones...

We were the object of all their attention. Was it the beauty of Ariane or the couple of young lovers that attracted sympathies? Happy people radiate happiness, and it comforted me that I was finally living a wonderful life and that I made the right choice.

The restaurant consisted of a succession of small, vaulted rooms, which each housed five or six tables. The dim light was provided by candles that made the atmosphere very intimate. Before leaving, I had a last look at the painting depicting "El Águila y la Serpiente," which was a memory of the legend of the ancient Tenochtitlan, the magnificent city of the Aztecs, a jewel of architecture of this civilization. What had the conquerors of Cortes done?

Then I saw in its niche, at the bottom, "The Virgin of Guadalupe," who was revered not only by Mexicans, but many people of the Caribbean. Her smile troubled me. She seemed to send me a particular message, and I had the strange impression of having already seen her somewhere years ago.

Finally, I deciphered the motto inscribed on a panel of flamboyant colors: *En tanto que permanezca el mundo, no acabará the fama, the gloria of México Tenochtitlán*, which meant, "As long as the world will last, the glory, the fame of México-Tenochtitlan, will subsist."

Once more, admiring the passion of these people from the distant fatherland, I felt like a brother in arms, exiled. We shared the feeling of abandoned roots, pegged to our body like our soul.

Ariane settled in, light as a butterfly in my serious bachelor world. I got used to seeing her toiletries near mine in the bathroom, her clothes stored in the closet near mine. Her perfume invaded little by little all the space of my studio. We occupied our thirty-five square meters in less time than it takes to say. I was impressed by the way a woman can fill a space with nothing, but manage to personalize it into a new habitat. We agreed to some unforeseen expenses to do this, like buying two pairs of brightly colored curtains to dress the windows of our large living room, and adding two or three matching cushions on the sofa bed that folded during the day. I put a trestle board close to the one I used as an office so that we could work together. We put a coffee table and two comfortable armchairs in front of the television and two green plants in front of the window—a little extra crockery because I had been content with the minimum until then. We bought two large cereal bowls with our names painted in black on them and the Statue of Liberty painted red, and we placed them prominently on the kitchen counter. These two bowls represented in my eyes the good couple that we were, and the beauty of living together. The city represented the magic of the couple, and the freedom to move on with my life.

Ariane had a lot of records, tapes, and CDs that she listened to all day long, a little too loud, in my opinion, for me, who was used to silence. It was one of her little defaults that I probably would have to get used too. I read and wrote for hours in the evenings, and her music or soap operas, which she watched on television, bothered me, but I reprimanded myself to have a little tolerance. I refused to reproach her for anything, too happy to share her life.

We both worked during the day because she managed to get an acting job in a company, and we were irritable after work. The hours I took in the taxi were necessary because I took care of all the household expenses, as well as Ariane's expenses: hair, nails, makeup, perfume, clothes, and shoes. I did not dare ask her what she was doing with her own money, because I knew she was preparing to pay for her second year of study and her parents were not helping her financially because we lived together. I had the tact, therefore, not to ask her any questions of a material nature, for my feelings for her forbade it. I regularly left a few bills in the drawer of the little dresser without checking her expenses and reassuring myself once a week that enough was left. The money sometimes went very fast, but when I saw her come home with a new hairstyle, a new blouse, or a small scarf or handbag, I said nothing because I knew that all her efforts of coquetry were intended for me, and I appreciated that intention.

Our nights were full of tenderness and caresses. We made love softly. I always feared rushing it because I respected her more than anything. This modest respect, even after several months of intimacy, seemed veiled and virginal. I quickly realized that we should work on improving our comfort level as soon as possible, but for the moment, I lived in moments of dream and discovery. It was the first time that a woman settled permanently and totally in my life. I threw myself into the experience with the passion of novelty, and that passion inhabited me. Our nest of love was modest but temporary, and I swore that no palace of the Arabian Nights had as much love and happiness.

I read her a collection of Paul Géraldy, an old-fashioned poet whom I particularly liked. I recited, with closed eyes, this little poem which seemed to me to have been written for us:

Come in, here is the scattered and temporary room,
Where I was alone, where I lived while Waiting for you,
And my sorrow with its lamp and its cupboards,
And here is the portrait of my mother at twenty.
Here are my class summaries and my poets
My favorite discs, my Bach and my Shubert,
The new calendar where the day of your feast,
Is marked with a cross,
And here are my verses.

- You and Me, Paul Géraldy

THE UNKNOWN OLD MAN IN THE PARK

Lampshade

You ask why I stay without saying anything?
This is the great moment.
The hour of the eyes and the smile, in the evening,
And that tonight I love you infinitely!
Squeeze me against you, I need to be caressed.
If you knew all that goes up in my mind tonight,
Of ambition, of pride, of desire, of tenderness, and of
kindness!

-You and Me, Paul Géraldy

The coffee vendor passed in the morning, and in its aroma, spreading the curtains, I woke my beloved with kisses on her neck. She stretched with childish pleasure like a blessed cat. We had lunch together and went about our daily activities on weekdays. On Sunday, when I did not take Jorge's taxi, we enjoyed staying longer in bed, loving each other, talking about our future, and making plans that excited me.

I decided to make this little feline, that I tamed day after day, my companion forever. I wanted a family, children, a white house in the country, and a garden where we would have dinner in the evening and celebrate birthdays around a pool. My dreams were grandiose, and Ariane laughed with happiness. Sometimes we went to dine with Mario, who always reserved his best table for us when I was not on duty, and Clara sang us a nostalgic love song. We then returned to our cozy little nest.

September approached, and Ariane finished her interim period. She had fifteen days of total freedom left, but I could not leave the jobs that allowed us to live. I kindly suggested that she go visit her parents for at least a week, and I would join her the following weekend. She did not think long, but despite everything, the decision of her departure gave my heart an unpleasant pinch. We were going to be separated, and eight days was an eternity.

She seemed a little tired and nervous lately. In the morning she had no appetite, complaining of nausea. I thought she worked too much and needed a real vacation outside of New Jersey. So many events happened, and she worked a lot, and now the academic year was going to resume. She went to her doctor before leaving, telling me she would be in the clinic all day for medical examinations. I was alarmed by this news, cursing my schedule that did not allow me to accompany her, but she reassured me.

"It is really nothing, my darling, a lack of trace elements, calcium, magnesium, but the doctor wants certainty," she said. "A little weakness, anemia perhaps, and then I will go to rest with my family. In a week you will find me in good shape. My mother's kitchen will cure me, you know! So, do not worry. I am not worried."

Things went as she predicted, and I was able to free myself for two hours to take her to the train station on a Friday night. Her drawn features told me nothing good. After her hospitalization, she had a stomachache. Her periods were often painful, and I felt stupid, helpless to relieve her. "The mystery of the woman." I returned alone and with my mind preoccupied. I missed her already and our apartment seemed too empty and too quiet. I waited impatiently for news of her safe arrival and began counting the days that separated us.

I went out to buy fruit at the local store, which closed very late. A golden twilight began to twinkle with pinkish clouds, and the park that saw the heat of this beautiful autumn day languished under its foliage that began to turn yellow. I slowly crossed the quiet street, deserted by children enjoying the last days of vacation, and continued past a charivari of unruly sparrows. Lovers were strolling there and exchanging kisses that make me think of Ariane. I knew that she was resting and having pleasant moments with her parents and siblings, all gathered together in the family home.

I called her several times a day and at night before going to bed to tell her "I love you" and to dedicate to her my most tender thoughts. The first two days, she seemed tense, but now I felt better. She really needed to recharge with her family. How much I regret not being able to do the same.

I promised to try to go to Port-au-Prince next year. The date of my naturalization was approaching. In two months, I would become an American citizen, and my dream would continue to grow. Another project was emerging, asserting itself little by little. I knew Ariane for several months and lived with her for three months. I knew that it was her that I wanted and not another. It would be easier to marry her. This idea made me a little afraid, but it was my dearest wish. However, would she accept? Apparently, she shared my feelings, and the life of two did not weigh on us, quite the opposite.

I decided to talk to her parents about having a wedding this year or next. I wanted to have enough money to have a beautiful family, while giving my future wife an unforgettable wedding party, like a fairytale. The idea of finally having a family and children moved me deeply. My sweet Ariane, you made me so happy!

I saw him on the bench. The old man, with his head looking sideways, wearing the same backward baseball cap, not saying a word. He suddenly came to my mind like a picture or a painting that I'd seen more than a dozen times without paying attention. Usually, he gave some seeds or crumbs to the pigeons or sparrows around him. This man was here every day without exception. He slowly looked up at me when I walked past, and the faded blue of his eyes made me a little uncomfortable. I looked away, but an imperceptible smile—or was it an illusion, a game of shadow and light in this twilight? —passed on his wrinkled face. I knew he was there every day, so I should say hello, but something held me back. His eyes looked like clear water, and I had the impression that he could not see me, or at least he could not see my physical appearance. I had the impression that he saw me there.

When I come back from the store, the old man carefully folded the bag of Kraft paper from which he was pulling seeds, and his eyes again dwelled on me. This time he was frozen, impassive. The night fell. I hastened to call my fiancée and announce my arrival in a few days. Why did this old man bother me so much? He looked like a ghost, a being without substance, only his cap looked real. I did not even notice how he was dressed, and he continued to look at me. I closed the door a little intensely. What was happening to me?

"Hello? It is Benjie. Good evening. How are you?"

Pastor Thomas, Ariane's father, was on the line. "Very good, my boy! What about you? Are you still working a lot? ...Oh, OK. Delighted to welcome you. I prepared a speech on the teaching of the parable of the 'Good Samaritan.' I will be glad to have you among my flock... and to beat you in chess after dinner," he added maliciously. "I'll get Ariane!"

A silence ensued, then it was the voice of his wife who answered. "Hello? Benjie, good evening. I am sorry, but you called a little late. Ariane and Patricia went out for a walk, and they have not come back. I guess they dined with their friends somewhere because they warned me not to wait up... Are you coming Sunday? Perfect, I will prepare donuts. I will tell my daughter. She will be happy with your arrival and disappointed to have missed your call. See you soon!"

A feeling of bitterness came over me as mechanically my eyes fell on the clock in the kitchen where I noticed that the needle was almost nine o'clock! It was the first time that Ariane had not answered my call. I found the hour late in relation to her habits, and then I was angry to let this nasty thought invade me. Was I losing my mind? Ariane was on vacation and it was normal for her to enjoy it and go out with her sister.

On Sunday, as planned, I arrived by car, and was received by my angel, babbling and tending as usual. She looked more rested. We spent a great day with the family, but I suddenly refused to reveal my intentions of marriage, convinced that it would be tactless not to mention the idea to Ariane first. She was frank and self-sufficient enough for me to marry her before talking to her family. We would have our celebration of love first. I then realized that I had not had time to buy a ring, something I promised to secure in a few days.

That evening, a young man came to the door and greeted the whole family as an old friend. I was introduced to him. Martin took Ariane in her arms and twirled her, laughing, dipping her head back. I'm told he's the mechanic of the family. Martin was Jamaican, almost as tall as me, well built, with a mischievous air, like a little boy. However, I had the impression that my presence did not delight him. Contrary to my open and communicative character, I found him unfriendly, forcing his laugher, and acting too familiar with Ariane, talking while stroking her arm, her hair, her hand. Was it the fact that we were separated for ten days that made me scowl? Jealous, yes, jealous. I would have preferred that she had eyes and attentions only for me.

Shut up, oh my pain
And leave me alone.

I preferred to get on the road again that same evening in order to get rid of this intruder as soon as possible. Ariane pouted a little, and her parents questioned my decision because they knew I was not working the next day. I pretended I had to work late in the house. I wanted to get my angel away from the one I perceived as a danger, but I felt very upset when my fiancée gave him two big kisses to say goodbye. She slipped our phone number and address to him. "Come see us in Roselle," she said. "You will be welcome, and Benjie works so much that you can keep me company."

No, he was not welcome, but what could I do? Was he just a friend of Ariane and her family?

My exasperation was at its height when he cast a scornful look on my repainted car. "You should change cars, old man, this one is a little old-fashioned. I can get you a price for a small cabriolet that has a folding hood, unlike this one."

His smile seemed to me that of a hyena and I answered him, at the same time, "I work with someone who can also get me another car, but you see, it is not *our* priority right now."

I stressed the "our," allowing Ariane to witness, but she did not flinch, absently taking refuge with her luggage in my Lexus. My fiancée fell asleep during the trip, and I respected her rest. We could not have a real dialogue until the next morning.

When I woke her gently under the sheets, happy to have her all to myself, she said, "Please leave me alone, Benjie." It was the first time she refused me, and I was stunned.

"But, darling..."

"I said, leave me alone. Don't you realize I cannot have sex?"

I did not understand, so she told me that her hospitalization was due to an abortion.

I could not believe my ears. "Why abort? It is a crime! You are a Christian, and I do not mind having a child with you, on the contrary!"

"I do not want a child right now," she said. "I am just starting to live. I want to be free, and we are not married, that I'm aware of! I am a modern woman."

Her harsh tone and fulminant eyes left me perplexed. "My love, you should have told me," I said. I wanted to tell her I was waiting for permission to ask her to marry me.

I knelt in front of the bed, trying to erase the feeling of dread that overtook. I kissed her hands. "Darling, never again, please," I said. "You killed our child. I must forgive you, but you really should have told me. Let's get married, it will be easier. What would your parents say? Your father, a pastor...?"

She turned and burrowed under the sheets. "Leave me for the moment. You are too naive. You live in another world, you poet! I have my feet on the ground." I was in pain and suffering. Nothing happened as I imagined. This demand for forced marriage, precipitated by circumstances, had a taste of gall rather than honey—a haven of the romantic setting I imagined, of her emotion when she would have answered "yes" to me. This was only a bad moment, I imagined. She suffered alone, too. Blind as I was, I did not foresee any of this. Her nausea, her fatigue. Who was I to reproach her instead of comfort her and share the burden? I was remorseful.

The days passed, and our life continued on its momentum. I had not spoken of the marriage, under the influence of the news that Ariane had announced to me, and our extenuating circumstances and excuses. She was preparing for her second year of study, and I, too, was about to face all my obligations—the work that allowed us to live, the studies I continued in the evening. I knew that the year would be more difficult because I would no longer have the additional income provided by the taxi. We would live on my salary because Ariane did not mention the possibility of having a job on the side. I had some savings that should help us.

I was happy to resume classes. I decided to go further in my studies, and I attended an advanced literature course, which proved that I had the ability, that English became a perfectly mastered language for me. My grades were getting better, and I was hoping to finish this university course and finally register (full time the following year) with the help of a scholarship.

I was not worried about Ariane's future, who was also doing well. We would soon be out of the woods. The idea of marrying her came back to taunt me. I absolutely wanted our relationship to be clear to us, and to everybody's eyes. I did not mention the abortion, so as not to disgrace her. She had many friends on the university benches, and from time to time, we received a call from Martin, who was would pass by and visit us. The problem was that I resumed my job at Mario's in the evening, so I was not there when he came. It was not my not being there that bothered me the most, of course, but knowing that he spent the evening with my fiancée.

THE DEPARTURE OF A RIGHTEOUS MAN

Because of these unfortunate incidents, moments of silence and reprobation ensued in our lives. I no longer alluded to the interrupted pregnancies or the nocturnal exits of my wife, and I never used the word "my angel" when referring to Ariane, pursued by the words of the unknown old man, "Lucibel," or "Lucifer."

The pressure of final exams was increasing. Ariane finished her course very honorably. I did, too, but I still wanted full-time studies and took steps to get a scholarship that would help us survive. We had been married for over a year, but were almost stuck in the routine of my in-laws: monthly meals and little daily problems. The honeymoon was short-lived.

The news of my father's poor health was alarming, and I prepared my heart for mourning. I went alone to the bedside of my dying father in time to seize his hand before he passed. I helped my devastated mother and my brothers complete the formalities of the funeral.

I saw his high stature when he returned from work, and the wicker chair where he settled for the evenings on the terrace. I thought back to the fabulous stories of his travels that filled our childhood with mysterious worlds to discover. I traveled the streets of our city where, accompanied by my mother and siblings, people respected and greeted him so many times.

I noticed in the church crowd an old lady dressed in white, leaning on a richly ornamented cane. She stood a little behind and did not take her eyes off me. I asked one of our old cousins if she knew her, and she simply replied, "That is Calixte, Benjie. She watches over you and yours... she is powerful, and the spirits obey her."

In my sorrow, I did not dwell on the words of condolences from poor old Petronilla, who would visit us from far away when we were children, which no doubt she no longer enjoyed since her husband had succumbed to a serious illness. I hugged the old Domitian, who was still alive, broken in two by her rheumatism. I was surprised to see charming Heloise who, holding a young child by the hand, sported a round belly, presaging that the second would arrive shortly.

Among the men in front of the church door stood Benny, my former classmate, a young man with his eyes downcast. Noéliane was there, a few months pregnant, and her doe gaze had the same sweetness. All of them—friends, relatives, neighbors—came to express their sympathy for the respected and proud man who had gone to other shores, and to support my poor mother, broken by sorrow.

My wife did not want to come. I did not have the courage to linger beside my family, and I felt the need to escape the demonstrative effusions. My life was continuing elsewhere. Did I still have a place in this world? I was already a stranger, at least by my new American nationality. My mind was tortured, and I could not seem to exteriorize my pain.

I quickly boarded the plane back to Newark, tearing myself hard from my mother's arms in tears. I arrived home, eager for rest and tenderness. Ariane was not at the airport waiting for me, so I had to take a taxi. I thought she was preparing a meal to welcome me and that she would surround me with her loving arms. Maybe then, I could cry my life away.

The house was calm and silent. On the small chest of the entrance, there was a note scribbled by her hand: *Excuse me, my darling, but Joan invited me out and would not take no for an answer. There is chicken and salad in the fridge. See you later. May I kiss you? Ariane.*

I did not know when she returned because I collapsed on the couch and fell asleep after taking a sleeping pill to clear my mind. Tomorrow would be another day. Frivolous butterfly, superficial child, Lucibel, or Lucifer? She haunted my heavy sleep. The choir sang a gospel that tore my heart, and I did not want to sing with the others. I felt lonely, lonely pain.

The eternal will keep you from all evil He will keep you in eternal life...

Our brother Zechariah has joined the stay of the just...
Pray my brothers for his soul and our sins.

Ariane's parents showed great compassion, and Thomas gathered the faithful of his parish the following Sunday to talk about the resurrection and comment on the miracle of Lazarus. His sympathetic words gave balm to my heart. Ariane cried when we got up to sing and give thanks to the Lord, asking him to bless the name of my late father. I heard his name repeated: "Zacharie." For me, it was always "Papa," nothing more. I heard that name too much in the past few days, and I wanted to bury it in my heart. Observing Ariane stealthily, I asked myself if her tears were sincere. She only met my father once. Fortunately, I had an answer to this question when Martin came forward to offer us his condolences, and my wife took refuge on his shoulder to pour out her sorrow.

Nothing is ever acquired man neither his strength nor his weakness and when he believes to open his arms His shadow is that of a cross.

- Louis Aragon

How many crosses did you have to bear, daddy, and how much did you leave me as an inheritance? I did not say goodbye because your tall figure, your smoking pipe, your wise advice, and your way of saying the things of life will be with me forever.

THE HARDER THEY FALL (HARDEST WILL BE THE FALL)

Life digs before us a gulf of all the caresses that have failed

- Félicien Artaud

    I was meditating on this text by Félicien Artaud, bringing my life closer to this gulf of emptiness. Weeks passed since I found my wife coming out naked from our bathroom in front of one of her male friends, and yet I avoided the problem. She came home late that evening and went to bed as if nothing happened. Since then, I was consumed in doubt, but at the same time, in the paradoxical hope of picking up the pieces of universe that I had begun to build.

The warnings of "well-intentioned people" failed to convince me of my blindness and irritated me, on the contrary. I made a fool of myself when Justin confided to me one day about seeing Ariane on Park Avenue.

"I saw her, Benjie. She was in a car with someone and had her arm around his shoulders while he was driving. She put her head against his at a red light, but they did not notice me. Cousin, be careful, you are too naive and sensitive. You live in your dreams, you know. I did not want to believe what I had seen myself."

Even then, I felt I needed more overwhelming evidence. These actions did not really matter, in my opinion. Friendship, tenderness, sympathy... there could be so many other explanations than the one they wanted me to believe. *Je ne voulais pas.* I did not want to give in to the dangers of denunciation.

I tried to be more considerate. I dared not ask her, "Do you love me?" I respected her desire not to have sex for the time being. However, I told her every morning when I woke up, "Hello, I love you," with a kiss on the neck and a cup of coffee.

The axe was thrown at me the day I told Ariane that I informed my boss that I would be leaving work at the end of the summer. I was happy because I obtained the university scholarship I applied for. This meant a certain lack of earnings and that we would have to live a little harder, but Ariane was going to look for a job.

The open window let in the sweetness of this June night. I prepared a good meal and wore a new blue shirt (she liked blue) while waiting for her return. I placed the university's letter prominently on the table so that she could read it and rejoice with me. I brought her a little bouquet of white lilac, which perfumed the room.

At eight o'clock, she arrived, graceful in her printed blouse with a dancing step that seduced me nearly four years ago. I prepared an apéritif for her. She put her keys and bag down and gave me a brief kiss of greeting, then went to the bathroom. Had she noticed the table set up, the smell of my curry chicken floating in the kitchen, the flowers in the big vase? I uncorked a bottle of red wine and waited for her to come out for dinner.

"Well, is it curry?" She asked. "I am not very hungry. Give me something to drink."

I obliged her request and told her to take a seat. She saw the mail from the university.

"What is this paper? Put it away, we're having dinner," she said.

I took the opportunity. "Look, darling, I received the scholarship I applied for. I am going to start a real university career. I warned Antonin that he will have to look for another worker at the end of the summer—"

"Oh, well, how will we live? That is ridiculous," she interrupted. "You need your job."

"Ariane," I said patiently, "We talked about this often, you remember, I hope? I have to make sacrifices to finish what I started. Working for Antonin is not my life goal. I will not remain an employee."

"What about me? I wanted to enroll for a second semester. With my experience, I am never going to get a management position. I must have at least a master's degree in communication and management, you know that."

"My darling, you can resume classes later, or do them part time."

"No, you think only of yourself. The sacrifices... I am feed-up with this!"

I did not want to irritate her, but I found her reaction unjust and inconsistent with what we had always agreed upon. "Ariane, stop getting upset, let us face the reality."

"Stop yourself. I do not want to go back to work for you, I am warning you. After all, you have to talk to me. I'm married to you. I'll always remind you of this, and you'll have to hear it whether you like it or not."

She began to raise her voice. She blushed with anger and clenched her fists, and I suddenly found her ugly, like a harpy. Her hair was disheveled. She stood in front of me, almost threateningly. I felt annihilated, speechless.

"What will you study? Ah, yes! Literature is an exciting subject, and you will get a very useful job!

If you were going to be a doctor, a dentist, or a business manager, I would understand! But *monsieur* wants to study poetry! That is how you will make a living? Let me laugh! Ha, ha, ha!"

Her wickedness and scorn in these words hurt me deeply. My sweet Ariane, I could not believe that in front of me was the moving angel whose modesty and smiles held me in slavery.

"Anyway, think. I will not accept this, and I will not live like a perfect housewife. I'm going out. I need to decompress, and you better think about this before tomorrow."

On these last words, she grabbed her bag, pulled out her cell phone, and ostentatiously called Martin, who must have been passing through New York. She played the tragedy of the scorned woman.

"Hello, Martin, please, come and get me...Yes, I will explain... No, he is here, but not for long. Believe me, things are going to change! Thank you, my dear, I am waiting for you."

A little courage came to me. "Ariane, if you leave, you will not come back here. It is over!" I said that hoping she would change her mind, and the nightmare would stop all at once.

She retorted with a sneer. "That's it, yes. Well, I am telling you that this is my home, too, and that I can do what I want. If you're not happy with it, then you pack your bags."

She went to the bedroom, and I heard her foraging in a vanity case where she threw some toiletries and makeup. Twenty minutes later, Martin honked downstairs. Recovered, dressed in a red outfit that I had never seen, she left unhurriedly, her perfume passing provocatively by me—the little crystal spray I gave her for her birthday—then slammed the front door. Her scent took me by the throat.

I felt paralyzed, but I turned to the window to look out into the street. Martin was waiting, smoking a cigarette, leaning against the door of a new black and white convertible. I saw my wife throw herself around his neck and cuddle into the arms of her savior and Don Juan. Lightning struck my head.

THE SHIPWRECK, A DESSEFRED SONG

Your memory arises from the night
I am The River to the sea knots its stubborn complaint.
Abandoned as the docks in the morning It's time to leave,
you abandoned it. (...)
You have engulfed everything
As far as the sea, like time.
In addition, everything in you was a shipwreck. (...)
Anxiety of pilot and fury of blind diver
Drunkenness of love, everything in you was sinking.
My winged, wounded, in the childhood of mist lost
explorer, everything in you was shipwrecked.

- Pablo Neruda

Can we accurately describe the sinking, the descent into hell, the dive toward the night? I suffered from the anxiety of failure. I did not know where to turn. I ran into sudden silence. My pain remained cold. I wandered in the deserted apartment, as though in pain. My surroundings only appeared to change when I heard car horns beckon from the street. I had no strength to look through the window at the admirers and friends who came looking for her.

We just passed each other. Ariane ignored me, but played nasty tricks that made my life impossible. She removed my dirty laundry from the washing machine, leaving only hers. The food was stored on separate shelves of the refrigerator. I slept on the couch, curled up like a fetus deprived of the maternal bunny refuge. The room was her domain and sometimes she locked it before going out. My toiletries were often thrown on the floor, and she kept the furniture in the bathroom. One day, I found my mail in the trash by the entrance of our building.

A thousand-and-one details of everyday life made our coexistence unbearable. I would return in the evening to find four or five people in the living room, drinking, smoking, and listening to loud music. Then everyone would leave to enjoy the pleasures of the night; I did not know where. I did not have a place to rest, sit down, or sleep, and I had to wait until they left to drop myself on the couch. I was tired. I did not sleep anymore and ate very little. Sometimes I knew they were talking about me in low voices and laughing, but I did not do anything because I was a ghost. Here, I was like a stranger in my own home.

By cons, I had to pay the bills that continued to arrive in my name. I saw on my bank statements that my wife did not bother to make withdrawals on my account since she still had the power of attorney, but that she used the credit card. I did not react or fix the situation because, maybe deep inside me, I still had hope that she would come back to me.

Lord, I was crazy, crazy with love, crazy with grief that undermined me. I telephoned Thomas, my father-in-law, to talk to him as a pastor, and confide in him about the situation. What did he say? He did not know how to help me and found himself distraught.

"Yes, the city has rotten my little girl," he said. "She has changed so much that I do not recognize her. Give yourself to the Lord, my son, and I will pray for you. The whole family is very disappointed."

I asked him if Ariane ever went to their home, since we lived apart yet under the same roof.

"Yes, she often comes to spend the weekend."

"Is she alone?"

"Yes, I think. She is often with Martin, but I think they are only good friends. I do not know."

Thomas looked hesitant, embarrassed. I did not want to make him feel uncomfortable and told him that it was better for Ariane and I to divorce. I thought I had the idea first, but to my surprise, he told me that she had already seen a lawyer.

Indeed, a few days later, she spoke to me, handing me documents.

"You have to sign this. I'm asking for a divorce, and you need to look for another place to live."

"But why?" I asked Ariane. "How did we get here, Ariane, please...?"

I started to cry like a child. Finally, I let go of everything that I held back for months: pain, frustration, extreme emotions. Nothing seemed to affect her.

The lawyer claimed alimony and the payment of rent. I was an employee, and she was a student working on her masters. She was working part time at Macy's in Willowbrook Mall. I learned that she resumed working for the holidays, but that she had no other means of support. She was declared a student. What about me, then? What was I?

I realized that nothing could save this marriage. My angel did not love me anymore, and I was getting worse and worse every day. I bent to her will and decided to take only the bare minimum. I abandoned our nest of love, hoping that my cousin Justin would host me a few days. I needed to be alone with my loneliness and heartbreak.

(...) everything in you is shipwreck, shipwreck, shipwreck.

I do not like it anymore, it's true, but maybe I love it.
It's so brief love but forgetfulness is so long

- Pablo Neruda

MYGALE

El Desdichado

I am the dark, the widowed, the inconsolable,
The prince of Aquitaine the tower abolished:
My only star is dead and, my constellated lute,
Carries the black sun of Melancholy. (...)

- Gerard of Nerval

It was with the rhythm of these sad verses that I crossed through the door of the classroom that morning, where I began to study the rudiments of literature, in addition to American civilization, but as a free listener, to prepare for my future studies.

I met my colleague, Mat. Eyes radiant, his complexion soft, Mat smelled the cup of coffee he was holding with delight. He held out his hand for a vigorous handshake. I always envied his radiance, his smooth appearance, as if everything could slip off of him, but I also wondered what kind of problem might have inconvenienced him. In life, everyone smiled on him. What gods bent over his cradle, when they seemed to have condemned me to despair? He studied idlily to pass the time and acquire a diploma to make his family happy.

Mat was always enthusiastic and optimistic, sure of himself, and brilliant. He was the one who mobilized attention and everyone listened, the one who sang salacious jokes, the one who cumulated female success, and always had the right friend in the right place when he needed it. I never heard that he had problems at the end of the month to pay his rent. Moreover, he lived in a superb loft that had no measure with the two-room kitchen, bathroom, balcony that I was living in with Ariane. Our nest of love, waiting to be improved as I tried to climb to the top of the ladder.

His stories told memories of different countries and continents. We did not know what his parents did, or exactly where he was from. Everyone imagined he had a good fortune, and his father had to be some international business leader or U.S. ambassador. Exotic countries. He never spoke of his family, and we respected his silence on this subject. I felt honored, as the poor immigrant student who struggled to make ends meet, by his friendship, and I was happy that our women grew to become almost inseparable. In fact, Mat and Joan lived as a couple without being married. According to Ariane, she and Joan were real friends.

My sad air must have intrigued him, because instead of heading to his classroom, Mat looked at me and said, "So, buddy, what is going on? You don't like your breakfast? Why the long face? Ah, yes, excuse me, you lost your father, I offer you my sincere condolences. It was so sudden for us. You did not tell us he was so sick."

"No, it does not matter... I did my mourning. He has suffered a lot, so maybe it's better this way. His death afflicts us, but it is a liberation for him and for my poor mother."

My voice was shaking a little, but I did not want to dwell on this subject. "Tell me, Mat, did you go away for the weekend?"

"Yes. Joan needed a change of scenery, and you know after my incarceration with Nelly (Mat said these words with a complicit wink), I could only oblige. Three days in the mountains. Charming inn, walks on the lake, it was the whole package!

Mat began to laugh and told me in confidence, "She is great in bed, when she wants to be. I know I'm wrong to try my luck with someone else, because we get along well. I am a bastard, my friend, a real bastard, because I do not deserve her." He laughed again.

I could not share his good humor and hilarity. Dark shadows invaded my mind. My mistake was to show it on my face because he looked very serious. "Poet, my friend, something is wrong. Are you having more problems with Ariane?"

I openly shared with him my disappointment following the behavior of my wife.

"Tell me everything," he said. "Looks like you have seen a ghost."

Ghost, yes, he had no idea. I was being haunted by a ghost—one who invaded my dreams, betrayed me, lied, and practiced adultery. I was the one who fell from the summit of happiness, abolishing my confidence and giving rise to disillusionment, pain. "The widower, the inconsolable...." My heart was tight, but I held back my tears. "I dreamed in the cavern where the Mermaid swims..." I dreamed, I dreamed.... Mermaid, my mermaid... My mind was confused. "The flower that pleased so much my sorry heart." Its petals were tinged with red shame and betrayal.

I finally found the courage to say, "She spent the night away. I thought she was studying with Joan, or simply visiting your home. She left me a note telling me that she was with your girlfriend and that she felt lonely. When I arrived from the airport, she was not there (and I think she did not come back until late the next day). I took a sleeping pill, so I do not know. I called, but a stranger answered her cell... or I dialed a wrong number. I do not know anymore. Everything is foggy in my head, and I never take pills. And then, she told me she was at a friend's house. I do not know who this person was, and she didn't come home because they had a party and got a little drunk. You know, she never drank before. I was in mourning, meanwhile she was partying. I do not understand anything anymore. This is the second time she told me that she spent the night at your home while you were away. The first time I had doubts, but this time you confirmed it yourself."

Mat seemed aghast. He leaned on a desk, swaying his legs and drinking some of his coffee, which he allowed to cool. "Wait... it is true that we did not have to leave, since Joan is preparing for her exam. I offered the trip last minute, but she did not hesitate to agree because she had nothing planned for this weekend. Moreover, Ariane suspected that eventually we would plan a getaway this week, so we would not be home. She is hiding something."

Mat stared into my eyes. "Benjie, be on your guard. I do not like a few of their friends." He did not add anything.

I started to think fast because I came to the obvious conclusion that she wanted me to discover this relationship. To challenge or provoke me? She wanted me to have no more delusions of our love. I remained silent, emptied from within for a moment before stating this obviousness to my friend. "She betrayed me deliberately and wants to make me suffer."

I felt Mat's palpable embarrassment and curiously wondered if he was capable of compassion or whether his superficiality was not just an appearance.

"Tell me, you know something. Joan and Ariane are friends, so... did you know?" I asked.

"No, no, what are you talking about? They do not share those kinds of secrets." Mat looked uncomfortable. "Listen, that's your own idea, or she's planting that idea in your head. You are still newlyweds! Pull yourself together—it is just a bad stage after a quarrel between lovers."

The Prince of Aquitaine, his tower in ruins. I see her face buried in Martin's shirt, shedding tears of deceit and falseness. I would have liked to believe her story, but I knew the heartbreaking and deadly reality. The tower of my happiness had thus collapsed—one I had built passionately out of stone.

Mat goes on without noticing. "When we see you together, you are in love like the first day you met. You embrace, you kiss..."

"Exactly. I kiss. Not her."

Mat looked desolate, anxious. "I am sorry Benjie, I still cannot believe it..." He added after a short moment of reflection, "Relationships are so complex. Who can know exactly what is going on? I do not know what to tell you. This will pass, damn it, you married her. It is not a small adventure. Do you want me to talk to Joan?"

"No! No! Let me fix it myself. Thank you!" I had the frightening vision of being stuck, paralyzed in the web of a spider. Ariane's webs closed around me, condemning me to a slow death under the effect of a venom that I identified as aspersion, distilled drop by drop into my own heart, poisoning myself.

When I passed in front of him, the old man raised his head abruptly. His sky-blue gaze seemed intrigued at the sight of this great, usually dynamic young man with his head down, his back hunched as if he bore tons of human misery on his solid shoulders. This young man walked with a hesitant step, and suddenly, as if drawn from his melancholy by the familiar look of the old man, he smiled weakly as if to apologize for showing weakness. "My only star is dead, and my studded lute carries the black sun of melancholy."

He just nodded and grabbed a handful of seeds for his birds. I immediately became aware of a particular fact. The pigeons usually coo, and the sparrows squeak, their noisy wings permanently agitated. That day, I felt like I was starring in a silent movie. The actors and the birds moved in silence as if they were spirits... Why was I afraid?

DOUBTS

From that day, I set up the ridiculous strategy of watching her, pretending to go to work, and unexpectedly returning home to surprise her, but that was a real torture. She still sported that mutinous, innocent look, humming in the bathroom. Nevertheless, we did not have any more real dialogues or laughs like before.

Several times, I came back too soon or too late. I often found young people at home, whom she introduced to me as classmates who came to study with her, without any hesitation. However, one of them, who was there most often, she introduced to me as Claude Carillon. He was Haitian like us, a nice slender boy, cordial in appearance, but I had trouble talking to him. I had nothing to say.

One of those mornings, I came home about an hour after I left. I opened the door as quietly as I could and snuck into the apartment. The morning sun was hidden by the curtains of the living room, and I heard slow music from a CD player. I smelled smoke, a blonde tobacco, but I did not smoke.

Claude was lying on the couch, a drink in his hand. He was smoking nonchalantly, his head turned toward the door next to the bathroom. His shirt was wide open on his shiny chest. His tie was undone, and loafers removed.

He saw me and leapt to his feet as if he'd been caught. I did not have time to question him, as Ariane came out of the bathroom, naked, still wet from the shower. She smiled to the angels and suddenly saw me. We were an odd trio on all three sides of the room. Me in front of the front door entrance; him, arms dangling, stretched out as if to jump out of the window; and her, looking a little distraught, motionless in her nakedness, offending me.

"What are you doing here?" She asked. "Aren't you working today?" She quickly regained control of her surprised look, and her voice was full of disdain.

She was the one who hurt me, but I was the one who felt embarrassed. I wanted to run to her, to throw my jacket over her shoulders to cover her.

"And what about you, are you not going to class?" I asked. I wanted to be a hundred feet underground.

In a detached tone, she answered, "I have to go. Claude came to pick me up. I did not want to take the bus." Her answer seemed absurd to me.

Quietly, pushing her hair back, a fine gesture that made her chest boldly protrude, she went into the room, sashaying her hips. I was mad with rage and paralyzed at the same time by her self-confidence. She thought I was naive.

I held back my anger, and I saw a smirk on the face of Claude, who, slipping behind me, went to the door and announced, "I am leaving, Ariane. I'll wait for you downstairs!"

Their nerve disarmed me, and five minutes later, my wife rushed out of the room. She was wearing a flowered dress that I loved because it suited her so well, heeled sandals, and red lipstick. She was holding documents under her arm. I wanted to seize her by the wrist in passing, but she slipped away and said very naturally, "You do not touch me! I will come back late. Have dinner without me."

"But we should talk! You were naked..." The words barely crossed my lips.

"No time, sorry."

I remained alone, motionless, my heart pounding, as if I were going to be sick. I felt like I was having a nightmare. I did not understand the scene that just happened, there under my roof. My wife walking naked, out of the shower, in front of another man. She, who often wore a mask of modesty. I thought painfully of moments of intimacy, where I had to turn off the light to touch her in the dark. The sensitivity she imposed on me when I had to turn around to avoid seeing her come out of the bathroom. I also thought back to times when she would cry when we made love, as if I were raping her. She shielded herself from some caresses with the excuse that she was a believer and did not want to be treated as an easy girl or a bad woman. How many times had I heard that speech?

At the same time, she aborted twice in a row. The reality was hard to pin down. Lucibel... Lucifer! She, my wife, in the guise of Janus, was two different people. It was inconceivable. I still wanted to wake up from this nightmare. In addition, the wake of her perfume filled my heart with despair.

I always persuaded myself that it would pass over time because she was so young and so inexperienced, at the beginning of her existence. I wanted to respect her, to tame her. Of course, we had been married for less than two years, but I had known her, in the Biblical sense of the term, almost two years before our marriage.

I thought back to our first embrace and realized that she was not a virgin at all, as she had claimed. However, my boundless love made me blind, incapable of judgment. Suddenly, recalling certain details, I realized that she fooled me at that moment. I remembered that we made the decision to marry because she said she was pregnant. I wanted to assume my responsibilities, so happy to have a child.

Finally, twice, during the last two years, she told the same story about supposed pregnancies. She said she did not want a child until she finished her studies. Material success took precedence over everything. She told me that each time she had an abortion without my knowledge. Just a few months prior, we fought because I asked her to explain to me how she, as a religious person, could commit the murder of her own children. The arguments went badly, and she did not speak to me for days. Instead, she went out frequently with her friends from the university, returning withered early in the morning. I did not recognize her anymore.

Then, I gave her a present. I took her out to a restaurant, and for a few weeks, things went back to normal. I was not happy, but she was there for me; it was the only thing that mattered. She had her band of friends from which I was excluded.

I was working more and more to save money to finally register for the next school year because she finished her studies in June, and it was understood that she would work while I realized my ambitions.

I regularly paid the rent, the house expenses, and her schooling. I opened a savings account and set aside the same amount each month to build my small capital. Several times, she asked me to take out money for futile expenses, like going on vacation or exchanging my old car for a shiny racing car like her dear friend Martin's. I retorted patiently that we could not afford it at the moment, not for at least four more years.

These explanations were also the impetuses for violent scenes on her part. She sulked for the entire evening or punished me by going out again and again with her band of inseparable friends, ignoring me for weeks. The fop, Martin, came looking for her in his cabriolet. He honked, and she ran down the stairs, as light as a flighty butterfly, without a word to me. I remembered one or two quarrels during which she screamed that I should not ask her to interrupt her studies and that she would not go to work or talk to me. Despite the cruelty of her words, I believed they were said on the back of anger, without really meaning it.

I made her aware of my plans from the beginning, and she had apparently accepted this compromise. This was what my daily life was, and many times, on the verge of annihilation, I promised myself to get things right with her. But when she came back, smiling at me, I was so happy to see her that I felt myself melt with forgiveness, saying to myself, it is normal, she is young. She must have fun with friends her age. Next school year, she will be in charge of the house and will have to work. She will be busy and will not be able to go out like now. Let her live carelessly.

So, I closed my eyes to all her extravagances; her friendships that I considered frivolous; her more and more provocative way of dress and makeup; her violent and insulting remarks; her caprices; her anger. I was so afraid of losing her, and I loved her passionately. I answered her advances for intimacy, but also obliged her refusals. She was the only mistress of our love embraces. I always bowed to her whims.

When we went out together, she replayed the role of the perfect lover and wife. My colleagues envied me because of this "wonderful" woman—so distinguished and sweet. She resumed her imitation of a girl who was discovering love and life. She let me take her hand, kiss her in public.

Sunday meals with her family were also the stage for this masquerade. However, for several weeks after lunch, Ariane took refuge in the kitchen, claiming she was helping her mother and sisters wash and put away the dishes. There were long meetings between them where men were not allowed. I stayed in the living room with my father-in-law, who asked me about my work and my future plans, or we played a game of chess and he showed me the hymns we would sing the following Sunday.

I wanted a quiet, drama-free life. That life shattered like an impure crystal. I was forever caught in the deadly webs of a poisonous spider.

The tiny recess into which I took refuge was freely given to me by Jorge. I did not want to live in Justin's apartment and clutter him with my morose air and my regrets. I continued to work not only out of habit, but out of necessity because I had to continue to support my ex-wife. The divorce was not final yet, but that was only a formality. I heard no news of Ariane for more than three months and did not want to receive any.

How did we get here? Things moved at a dizzying pace, and the words "it's over" and "divorce" sprung up. Who had pronounced them first? I did not even know anymore. The routine life, the conjugal habits, the walls of the hearth, collapsed in an instant.

After having the obvious proof of her betrayal, I had two suitcases packed in a few minutes, abandoning years of what I wished to call happiness and love. I lost a lot of money and my *joie de vivre*, and it was difficult for me to write because my poetry revolved around the obsession of betrayal and ransacked love.

THE END

I lost interest in everything and worried about of the imminent resumption of classes. How do I find motivation to progress and learn? But the worst was yet to come.

One morning, Antonin came to find me in the workshop where I was busy working. "Benjie! Oh, Benjie! I received a phone call for you before you arrived."

I raised my head. "What is it?"

Antonin looked embarrassed. "The police, you have to go to the police station before tomorrow. I said you would come later, to give you time to get ready."

"The police? What's the matter?" I did not have any tickets. "Did they tell you anything?"

"No, they just said it was personal."

"It is better if I don't wait and call them now, but I do not have my cell phone anymore. Can I call from here?"

"Of course, Benjie, and if you have to go right now, no problem."

I recalled the number Antonin gave me. I had a rather irritated inspector on the other end of the line who asked where I was now.

"At work, like usual."

"Do not move," he replied. "I'll come to see you. I must speak to you."

He refused to tell me more and hung up on me. I wondered what to do. Resume my work? Wait?

My anxiety was at its height. I took a cup of coffee into the boss's office to wait for the arrival of the police. I did not have time to enjoy this coffee because a few minutes later, bursting with loud sirens and flashing lights, two police cars braked brutally in front of the shop.

Four plain-clothed inspectors were already in front of me and, consulting a sheet, checked my identity. Not knowing what a search was like, I let them take my identity card and my pay stubs they had requested from Antonin, who was stunned. Then, coming at me like hawks, they handcuffed me, bringing my arms back unceremoniously. "Come on, man, we are going to the police station."

I tried to protest, but one of them drew a baton out of his pocket menacingly, then pulling me like a thief, they threw me into one of the cars. I had time to shout to my boss, "Please, warn my cousin and call my lawyer! It is Emerson, Greg Emerson. Justin knows his address."

I found myself in a very uncomfortable position between two men who were chewing gum and not speaking to me. I was driven like a criminal to the central police station in the city. I was dazed, and my arms and wrists ached. I felt anger and shame rising in me because I had been picked up at work, like a criminal, without even knowing what I was accused of.

We finally arrived at the police station. We went through the corridor, and then I was thrown behind a little gray desk. The place exuded gloom and dirt, and the only window facing me had a curtain yellowed by nicotine. The windows behind me were either shielded or covered with dirt, as they prevented daylight from entering. I wasn't sure.

I remained there, overwhelmed and dejected. Finally, an older man sporting a thin Clark Gable mustache appeared and sat in front of me. His hands were stuck in the pockets of his gray trousers.

"First name, last name, date and place of birth, nationality, job..." He asked the questions after opening a computer behind which he sat.

I protested, asking him what I was accused of.

"Answer the questions first," he said. I had the impression I was living in a bad black-and-white film from the fifties.

He had a brittle tone, a cruel air, and his black eyes looked at me without compassion. I gave him my civil status and reiterated my question, "Please, what's going on?"

"You are the subject of a complaint from your wife. Child abuse and abandonment, as well as domestic violence."

"Sorry?" I did not process everything.

He began again impatiently, "I said, complaint for child abandonment, abuse, and domestic violence."

"You must be mistaken, sir. I do not have a child, and I have not seen my wife in a long time. We are divorcing. You are not looking for me."

It seemed so obvious to me that even I breathed a sigh of relief. However, nothing phased my interlocutor. He was really stubborn.

"I have no time to waste. You will tell me everything, man, and you are not going to get away with it."

I continued to deny and repeat the same argument. "I have no child. This is crazy. I never hurt my wife..." The conversation was going around in circles, and the policeman did not want to quarrel.

I loudly proclaimed my innocence. "Finally, if I have a child..." (A doubt had crept into me, now knowing the evil Ariane) "...tell me if it is a boy or a girl. How old is the child? What is his or her name. I would like to know."

The policeman glanced at the dusty clock, whose round dial stared at me like the eye of a placid cow. "Anyway, it is time to eat," he said. "I'll let you think; otherwise; you will wait to see the judge. You are placed in custody from now on, since you will not cooperate."

I was mad with rage, but did not want to aggravate my case. He did not want to listen to me. He seemed deaf to all my denials. Besides, I was assailed by the same suspicions that plagued me already. Did Ariane have a child? I thought back to the carefully hidden abortions. Maybe she had kept a baby to enslave me, give me remorse, extort money, or just because the love was not completely extinguished? I tried to count the months since we last had sex, but she had left me and cheated. Could I be the father of her child if she had one? But, why would the lawyer not tell me anything when I set the amount of the pension I paid her? The situation became inescapable.

I was exhausted, thirsty, and hungry. I was alone in a cell with rough concrete walls. I had my handcuffs, shoes, and belt off. My pockets were emptied, but that was the only noticeable change in my situation. I looked forward to the return of the inspectors and the appeal of the lawyer or my cousin. I screamed and shouted, shaking the bars of the cell.

An unhappy guard finally appeared. 'You have a visitor. Approach here."

He took me out and handed me a small bottle of mineral water at the same time. My lips were dry. I promised to complain about the abuse and was pleased to see Greg Emerson, my lawyer, standing in the hallway. His meetings with the police lasted an eternity. Greg tried to reassure me, reading the details of the charges listed. He took notes feverishly and also protested from time to time. However, the police officer was a subordinate, unaware of my case. The inspectors I saw earlier that morning had disappeared.

Finally, he told me in a tone that did not allow any optimism, "Unfortunately, Benjie, I cannot do anything for today. It is Friday, it is past three o'clock, and the judge is not here. They must keep you until Monday. Your cousin is waiting for my call. I need you to tell me everything. Was Ariane pregnant when you separated? Did you ever touch her? Are you hiding anything from me?"

These remarks on his part saddened me. "I swear, Greg, I wanted to have a child so badly, but she did not. She would never have changed her mind when we separated. Maybe only to bother me. I cannot stay here, Greg, what can we do? As for beating her or making her suffer violence, you know me, I am quite incapable of it. I loved her so much. I endured everything for her, avoided arguments, so that she would come back to me, always. How can she tell such lies? We need to call her parents. Her father is a man of God. He knows me well, and he will confirm what I told you. What do I do?"

"Nothing for the moment, my friend. You will be treated well. There is no proof. I will see you Monday at eight o'clock. Justin will arrive. Sorry, Benjie, but she will pay dearly for her lies. We will not give up, believe me. You will be free as soon as we see the judge, even if we have to pay bail. Abuse of authority, misrepresentation, breach of public fame—we will ask for damages that she is not prepared for, trust me. And the police will also hear from me about their expeditious and violent methods. Hold on until Monday. Justin is going to bring you a radio, newspapers, and a book or two. I will ask for you to be moved to a more comfortable cell. Maybe the guard will let you watch TV with him. You are not a murderer. You are the victim. If it is not OK, call me. You will get a phone call tomorrow. I made arrangements with the old guy; he is nice. I will see you Sunday morning."

He pointed to an old policeman, tall, a little hunched. His eyes were pale, and he looked out the window, as if he were scanning the sky through the gray tiles. "I love birds," said the old man, in a low voice, as if talking to himself. "They have a beautiful soul."

The old man was so far removed from the image of a policeman—strong, young, well built, rough—but, he vaguely reminded me of someone.

He took care of me during my two days in custody so that I did not miss any water or meals. Indeed, he brought back the items that my cousin left me and offered to let me watch a football game on the TV near him. He did not speak much, but sometimes, he took a sympathetic look at me behind the bars of the cell where I was transferred, mentally sorry for the last months of my life, lying on a slender bench with a gray cloth, but not too dirty at first sight.

He was assisted by a young policeman who was not very talkative either, so I sat there and meditated for more than forty-eight hours on my deplorable fate, on the injustice, the deceit of the one I compared to an angel, whom wanted my ruin, my death. I cursed myself for getting stuck in the deadly webs of the one I now called "Tarantula."

DEATH OF MY SOUL

Drawing in the waves of despair, I lost all strength and fighting spirit. Although it was very easy, with the help of my lawyer and the testimonies from my boss, friends, and, unexpectedly, Ariane's family, to prove that I was the object of a horrible scheme. I remained disgusted, forever wounded by this story.

The police officers returned my things, and the judge was nice during the hearing, but it didn't erase the memory of forty-eight hours spent in a prison cell, this arbitrary arrest, police aggression, and public humiliation at work. Even when one is cleared of all suspicion, one cannot savor the victory because they are tarnished by so many other unforgettable things. I had no children. I never mistreated my wife. I always assumed my financial commitments. However, my honor was tainted. What could I do?

I sank into a sort of depression, even more prominent than before. I took a few days off to get my bearings. Was my life going to stop in the middle of the road? The university—my future was there. Locked in my tiny little room, I rehashed all these misadventures. I could not tell if I felt hate or love still for this fallen angel. Despite my ability to forgive easily, I could never rebuild the ash heap that Ariane left in her wake. How do I stay in this city and continue to live as if nothing happened? I could not bear to go passed our old apartment; to see the park where the familiar figure of the old man fed the birds. I reassured myself in my state of stress and depression of this chimerical man. I must be disturbed.

My natural survival instinct slowly caught on, and I had to move on. I asked the university to turn my scholarship into a study abroad in Paris or London. The mere fact of taking this step made me realize that I was beginning to recover and rise again.

I organized my affairs, which I had neglected lately, and asked my bank to supplement a scholarship in the form of a student loan. I regretfully had to leave my boss, Antonin, and Mario the owner of the pizzeria, who had both supported me unconditionally. I stayed with my cousin for another month. He was apologetic and compassionate. I avoided the tears and sorrows of my mother, who did not understand anything in these situations of misfortune. I packed my luggage in a hurry as soon as I knew that my request was successful. I was one of the students chosen to study in Paris. Nothing better could happen to me at that moment. I wanted to leave without looking back on my past of pain and affliction.

PARIS OF ALL MY DREAMS

Under the Mirabeau bridge flows the Seine
And our love
Is it necessary for me to remember it?
Joy always came after the pain

Vienna at night, rings the time
The days go away, I stay
(...) Love goes like this running water
Love goes away
As life is slow
And as the hope is violent.

Vienna at night, rings the time
The days go away, I stay.

- Guillaume Apollinaire

I often remember the last few months before my departure. I left the Newark airport the year before as a criminal, with his head down and heart heavy with regret. Grief sat on the edge of my eyelids. Hidden under dark glasses were my red eyes of insomnia. I turned one last time to look at the grandeur and madness of New York that disappeared in the clouds. I took another path, not as a conqueror, but as a wounded man fleeing his past. I went to Paris simply to forget. I wanted a reason to renounce, or to be reborn in the land of poets, in the city of lights. Where better to do this than the banks of the Seine, where so many famous writers had lived, dreamed, and produced so many immortal works that filled my schoolbooks?

During the entire flight, I bathed in a drowsy convalescent, although deep inside me emerged a new exaltation, growing every hour of flight that brought me closer to Paris, the mythical city that everyone wanted to see at least once in their life. I knew full well that the months that awaited me would not be months of laziness, and that I would have to study hard, succeed, and detach myself from homesickness. I especially needed to put distance between myself and New Jersey to erase the painful memories.

It was reassuring, however, to be expected. I had a host family: Mr. and Mrs. Deaunier. I wished with all my heart that we would get along well. I knew I would live in Maison-Laffitte, a nice neighborhood, a residential suburb. My only concern for the moment was for the immigration and university registration formalities to be carried out quickly; the distance between the Sorbonne and Nanterre.

I wanted to be exemplary in my studies and pay tribute to all those who gave me their vote of confidence. I saw the plane of this American company as my last link to my old way of life, with passengers who chatted in English and French. I crossed the Atlantic and freed myself from the culture that had been mine in recent years.

"Ladies and gentlemen, please fasten your seatbelts... Fasten your seatbelts... We are beginning our descent into the Charles de Gaulle airport. The temperature on the ground is 16 degrees Celsius..." I could not prevent myself from being moved by this announcement. Roissy, **Charles de Gaulle airport**, had mild weather despite the slight morning fog. Arrival formalities went quickly, and I easily retrieved my suitcases.

The Deaunier family was at the rendezvous behind the security fence at the airport. Mr. Deaunier was tall with easy-going hair and had a gray and sparkling look behind his rimmed glasses. Mrs. was a dynamic and laughing woman with bluntly cut auburn hair and blue eyes, whose kindness made me almost burst into tears. These unknown people who hugged me and welcomed me to French soil would be my family for the next few years.

Paris put on her autumn dress to receive me. I opened my eyes wide, wanting to remember forever these postcard images of the France's capital. The welcome outmeasured my expectations, and my attentive hosts made me take a long walk of recognition on the big boulevards.

I saw the Champs-Élysées, the Place de l'Étoile, the Concorde, the banks and river boats of the Seine, the Louvre, the Pompidou Center, and the Luxembourg garden, marveling at these magical places that I knew from readings, films, and songs without ever having set foot there. Mr. Deaunier's comments were interesting, concise, and of course, I made the promise to rediscover everything myself in the weeks to come.

I had a special fondness for Montmartre, an artistic place that moved me a lot. I would have liked to see more of it, but it was getting late. I did not feel tired or jet lagged; I filled my lungs with Paris air. "You, Paris, take me in your arms."

We ate in a very Parisian bistro, which enchanted me. I feasted on grilled bone marrow, sprinkled copiously with *Guérande* salt, butter sandwiches, and *gratin dauphinois*, washed down with a little Loire wine that I discovered. My experience in this area was summed up in Bordeaux, as the capital of French gastronomy, and the wines of Alsace, which I also heard about in Burgundy.

I felt reassured, relaxed, and already in love with France. This stay served to bury old ghosts. I wanted to forget the disappointment of the shattered marriage and heartbreaking divorce, and bring new light to my heart. Any wound eventually heals if it does not kill, I thought. You, poet, will no longer be the poet of cursed love, but that of joy and hope.

Autumn and winter passed, gradually dressing my wounds that were closing. I wandered the streets of the Marais now. I found my corner of reverie in the Luxembourg garden, and my little bistros, where I tasted a coffee and a croissant in the mornings when I did not have early classes. I was accustomed to the Sacred Heart, and I stopped at certain points of observation from the bridges of Paris. I loved to cross the Champ de Mars and look up like millions of tourists toward the noble Eiffel Tower by putting my hand at the level of my eyes to shelter them from rays of the sun. All these gestures, all these paths, were mine now. I felt adopted by Paris.

It was on the boulevard Saint-Michel on a Friday after school when I met Josselin. We went to get a beer a few minutes after meeting, leaning on the counter of Café Luxembourg, the bistro that I frequented, to relax before taking the RER. We admired the pleasant and elegant Parisians. Most of them, in fact, seemed more like strangers like me, rather than of old French origin.

I noticed that we, students visiting from elsewhere, modeled our behavior and image after the clichés we were taught about French manners. We wanted to be classy and well-dressed. We expressed ourselves in a distinguished way, all things considered. The students that I met on the banks of the Sorbonne, French who came from all the regions of metropolitan France, had neglectful personalities. Their activities were questionable, and they spoke a language that seemed barbaric to me, as it moved away from the purist rules of grammar that we were learning to obtain our degree.

Josselin was Haitian like me and studying history. I immediately liked his thunderous laughter and assured look. He was as tall as me, elegantly dressed, and possessed an optimism that I lacked— like he could conquer the whole world. He was a professional flirt, determined to take advantage of his stay in France. He reduced to his mercy any female who passed within his reach. He bragged about going out with a different woman at least every week, and told me happy adventures of husband cuckolds and clandestine relationships that were sometimes risky. He was always in love, but each time with a different girl. In fact, he loved the woman in all women and could not resist any smile or glance. That was his best quality and his greatest defect.

I put myself in his wake, judging that I had been too wise until then and not devoted enough time to the female conquest, which I absolutely had to win before the end of my stay. I went on several dates accompanied by Josselin, but, like the heron of the fable, none seemed interesting or matched my ideals. I was always looking for someone better, after furtive hugs that left me satisfied only at that moment in time.

No doubt I was still looking for the reflection of Ariane through each of these women. My relationship with Josselin actually changed my way of life. We went on beautiful walks, pacing the avenues and making our mark on the world, while glancing shamelessly at the girls we often passed. From time to time, we got a nice little meal at Café Luxembourg on Saturday evenings, while counting our meager savings that barely satisfied our needs. We also danced on Saturday nights, frequenting the Caribbean and especially *La Pointe des Antilles*, where we found the rhythms of the country and the heat of a punch or rum, not to mention the attractive girls.

One evening in Melun, we went to dance the "Skah Shah Number 1." It was April 11, 1998, and we came without dates. Josselin left his last girlfriend because she was too possessive, so we were determined not to return home alone.

Josselin immediately spotted two women sitting at the end of the dance floor. We went to get a table next to them. The white woman was dressed in black and had honey-colored hair in a supple bun. The other, a beautiful, mixed-race woman, had short hair that accentuated her perfectly round face. I admired how elegant she looked with this haircut. She wore a water-green silk dress that emphasized her complexion. Her almond-shaped eyes glanced at me two or three times, so I decided to go to their table and invite them to join us. They refused politely, but Josselin, after confiding to me that he was already pinching for the blonde, assured me that we would be successful. Without looking at the price, he sent glasses of champagne to our neighbors. They appeared surprised. The eyes of my chosen girl kept lingering on mine, so I decided to invite her to dance.

I took this stranger in my arms, and in a few seconds, she was the perfect complement to my body. We moved to the rhythm of the music. Her form married mine, and our steps agreed instantaneously. The dance was purely erotic expression, and I worried that this wonderful harmony would cause me to fall totally in love, there, on this dance floor. This woman I did not know made me vibrate from head to toe without control.

I got bolder and squeezed her harder. She seemed to also seek closer contact. My mouth against her ear, I wanted to whisper words of love, but instead I said, "My name is Benjie. What's yours?"

"Marie-Reine. My name is Marie," she answered.

"That's beautiful. Mary—a sign that you are already my queen!"

She laughed warmly and deeply, turning me on even more. It was a woman's laugh, not a childish or crystalline laugh. I was very affected by it.

Then I said, "Wait, I will be right back." I ran to find the bouquet that sat on our table in a small vase. She continued to laugh.

"I present you this bouquet that my hand
Just sorted out from these blooming flowers"

"Thank you. You say beautiful words... what a beautiful tribute!"

"Those verses are from Ronsard," I said. "I'm a poet, too, but you deserve better than me!"

The ice was broken, and, hand in hand, we returned to the table where Josselin and Marie's friend, Leah, were engaged in tender conversation. My friend didn't waste any time embracing Leah. I did not dare do the same with Marie, but her hands pressing against mine and her eloquent look were invitation enough, so I leaned toward her, finally putting my impatient lips on hers.

I was in love! That was confirmed. Mary seemed interested, but my natural timidity resurfaced, and I totally lacked self-confidence. How could this queen among women be interested in me? That evening, for the first time since my arrival, I had the impression that my life was going to change for the better.

We exchanged phone numbers when the club closed. Since we were in Melun, we had quite a long trip home. Josselin had just bought a superb Ford Fiesta, which would allow us meet again.

With my head full of the words I exchanged with Marie, still smelling the strong perfume that rose from her neck and wrists, I felt nothing but exaltation and mad love. I forgot all the bad memories and thought only of happiness.

"Time is running out, time is running out, my lady." Indeed, I was anxious to speed things up and hoped that my queen would quickly decide to call me. Should I rush destiny? The emotional loneliness that was my companion for the last few months was about to say goodbye, and I would not regret it.

On the way back, while Josselin was making plans for his next date with Leah, I remained rather silent. I felt stunned by the feelings that rose in me, and the joy prevented me from pronouncing coherent words. I daydreamed, but my past of romantic despair did not tire from attempting to undermine my happiness. Was my lacerated poet's heart finally going to heal from its wounds? "Oh, Mary, full of grace."

I was distracted the next day. I tried to focus on my coursework, but "The Thought of the Enlightenment" did not captivate me, and my soul as a poet was in effervescence.

Haitian friends organized a small party the same evening, and Josselin took me there almost by force. The evening was in full swing, but I did not have the heart to really enjoy myself. My spirit was preoccupied with the night before. My feelings were so strong for Marie, who I would probably never see again.

"Benjie, your phone keeps ringing. Are you going to answer?" Josselin asked me.

I realized I had left my phone in my jacket pocket on a sofa because, with the alcohol contributing, the temperature rose badly in the room where everyone was dancing, laughing, smoking, talking, and drinking.

I was a hundred leagues away in the hubbub around me, so I had trouble deciphering what Marie was trying to say. I went outside where I could finally hear her deep voice say that she, too, was thinking about last night and wanted to see me again soon. She asked me to get dinner with her the next evening.

She lived in Drancy, Boulevard Jean Jaurès, and would meet me at seven-thirty at the station to pick me up. How to describe my joy, my desire to jump, to cry, when I heard this invitation? I wanted to follow in the footsteps of Monsieur de Ronsard's letter to Hélène:

Live now, do not wait tomorrow Pick up today the roses of life. I decided to change my habits, on the verge of to embark fully on the adventure that held out my arms and to love my Queen, forever.

The day had scarcely risen, and I was already blackening pages of notebooks in homage to Marie, my beloved:

What grace and what shade In the sweet and seductive shine, You have the candor of a child And innocent rides Your eyes are the eyes of an angel Know as much without thinking, Reveal the desire of a strange man By an immortal kiss...

The verses followed each other, the poems chained together under the inspiration of my muse. I could not focus on anything, filled with impatience for dinner. I made sure to isolate myself all afternoon so that I could prepare for this fabulous occasion.

Mrs. Deaunier was, like I said, a second mother. There were two foreign students living in this beautiful house, a mansion, with stables because the family bred racehorses for decades. We each occupied a small, very functional and stylish apartment above the stables, with a nice dining area, a small private shower room, an office equipped with a computer, and a lot of shelves that served as a library. I enjoyed this rather unusual comfort for a student, thinking of most of my college colleagues who were housed in poorly-heated hovels without amenities.

I owed a lot to this welcoming and hospitable family. I could count on succulent meals every day with the family. The parties on special occasions were also an opportunity to meet their loved ones. Mrs. Deaunier knew how to organize a small surprise evening or a good family reunion with a refined dinner. She encouraged my studies and wished great success for my future. "Here is our future ambassador," she said, or, "You are our next Kofi Anan, Benjie." She truly believed in me, and my loneliness considerably softened by all this thoughtfulness; this family cocoon that I found; the solicitude of all the members of the family, parents, and children. Even today, their memory moves me, and I remain very attached to them, knowing that I am their forever guest almost ten years later.

MARIE-REINE, MY LOVE

I believe that love can last a lifetime
And the Heart can define when love is real
I think I can try my luck and say what I feel (...)

- *Tears of Love*, Lociano Benjamin

The journey from Maison Laffitte to Drancy seemed like an eternity. I was so afraid of a delay in the RER, a surprise strike, or any other incident that could thwart my journey, that I left early. The trip would take me about half an hour.

I jumped in the RER A towards Marne-la-Vallée, not bothering to sit because I did not want to wrinkle the plants of my linen suit. I was going for a casual, chic look because I did not know where we were going to dine. Approaching Chatelet, the station where I had to transfer, my heart was pounding. I had to catch the RER B Roissy, which should take me to Drancy. At seven-fifteen, I finally found myself on the platform of the station.

The wait began. I listened for every step of high heels and watched for each silhouette at the end of the platforms with worried, sweaty hands. I had the impression that people stared at me with suspicion as time went by. Soon it was seven-thirty, then forty, then fifty, and then eight o'clock. I was pacing up and down those damned platforms without daring to exit, in case she arrived on the other side. Shortly after eight o'clock, I decided to call her at the number I knew by heart. The number was a wink of destiny because the string of digits included my date of birth.

"Hello, who is this?" At the end of the third ring, this child's voice disarmed me. I did not expect to have a toddler at the end of the line, so I was speechless for a few seconds.

"Who is this?" The child insisted.

I recovered thinking I dialed the wrong number. "Excuse me, I wanted to talk to Marie-Reine, but I must be wrong..."

"Marie-Reine is my mom. Do you want to talk to her?"

"Yes, please."

"She is not here. Do you know her?"

"A little... I am Benjie. Do you know where she is?"

"No, I am with the babysitter."

"What is your name?"

"Jonathan. I am six, almost seven."

"Bye, Jonathan."

The song of Claude Francois played in my head, and I had the impression that the phone was crying, too. I felt helpless discovering that she had a little boy she didn't tell me about. But after all, I did not know anything about her. What did I have to be upset about?

Eight-fifteen. Should I leave? The grace period of waiting time was exceeded. Claude Francois' song still resonated in my head: *The phone is crying. You are not there...*

"Benjie, Benjie!" She ran along the platform as fast as she could in her wedge heels and red dress that was molded to her body like a goddess—the body that I pressed against me and that capsized my senses to the sound of the music. She wore big, gold hoop earrings that made her look like an African queen, and her hair was styled in a red turban, too She was radiant, and my love for her that seemed obvious was now undeniable.

She threw herself on me and waited for a kiss, but I looked at her and said, "Did you want to test my patience, or what? I have been waiting for you for almost an hour."

She did not answer me, and just said, "Kiss me!"

This invitation made me happy, but I was disappointed that she didn't answer my question. I wanted to say that I called her home, but I changed my mind. She will tell me everything herself.

I kissed her again and again, and she suggested going to dinner at a Japanese restaurant on the Boulevard Jean Jaurès where she lived. The strongest memory that I hold forever of her was the flavor and passion of our kisses.

This dinner lasted two hours at least, and we did not stop holding hands and looking into each other's eyes, intoxicating ourselves with each other. We wandered out of the restaurant to kiss more freely in the street. I never get tired of her hot mouth, her gaze drowned in mine. Time no longer mattered. We no longer saw the people or things around us. We walked in the darkness staring at each other, amazed at what was happening to us, and perceived only the present moment—the heat of each other, her perfume, the sweetness of her lips again and again.

The children who love each other kiss each other standing
Against the doors of the night
And the passers-by who pass by pointing their finger at
them.
But the children who love each other are not for anyone
And it is only their shadow
Who trembles in the night (...)
They are far more than the night
Much higher than the day
In the dazzling clarity of their first love
                                            - Jacques Prévert

Neither of us were each other's first love, but we discovered the stealthy fervor of teenagers.

I was very surprised when she asked me to come over to her place. Again, I wanted to ask her about Jonathan, but preferred to keep quiet.

I discovered Marie-Reine's three-room apartment. It was a modern building with a flower garden and luminous decor, a very feminine universe, designed in her own image. She made me sit on a blue sofa. On the wall were Haitian paintings: Sterling Brown and Joseph Thony Moise, AKA Titonton.

She offered me a glass of wine and cuddled against me on the couch. Finally, the secret was unveiled as she leaned toward me with worry in her eyes. "What if I told you I didn't live alone?"

"I do not know. I thought you were single," I said.

"It is not another man. I have a child, a boy, who's seven-and-a-half."

I did not look surprised and replied, "I know. I know about Jonathan."

It was her turn to be surprised, and she straightened up. "How do you know my son?"

I told her about my impatient phone call from the station. She relaxed and returned into my arms. We talked for about half an hour, and I learned that she was a lab assistant at Denfert-Rochereau.

Suddenly, the futile talk faded, and we kissed, which became deeper until our desire overwhelmed us. Getting up at once, she pulled me by the hand and led me to her room. We were feverish, and our impatient gestures were awkward as we removed our clothes. She had a feline flexibility and wrapped her legs around my tense body. She gave herself without restraint, without false modesty.

I threw her on the bed, and we make love brutally, passionately. She shouted her pleasure like no woman had ever done before. We did not succeed in satiating our hungry bodies, hanging onto each other as if we were shipwrecked. Her caresses left me no respite. We started again with more tenderness and calmness, discovering each other as attentive lovers.

"I love you," "I love you," "I love you," we repeated in unison. I wished I could stop time on these minutes of extreme happiness. I was so stunned, because after despair and loneliness, I finally saw the sky open.

IN PARIS WITH HER

My weekends were now completely filled with my new love and little Jonathan. The child waited for me at night so we could play together. On Sunday's, I took "my little family" on walks in the Luxembourg garden, and sometimes we took a boat to stroll along the Seine. I felt proud. I saw myself as a father. Sometimes I stopped to watch Marie-Reine walk in front of me. She looked so good. Her elegance and sensuality capsized the senses. We were a beautiful couple, and sometimes I felt envious looks from people. We shared the joys of each day, and our fevered nights reconciled me into existence.

Jonathan's father lived in Martinique and took him during the school holidays. Then, my lady was all mine. We went on a trip around France, which I began to discover with my band of friends the year before. Each region was a renewed delight. We began with Brittany and its rugged coastline and small fishing ports, whose names evoked my past readings: Saint-Malo, Saint-Brieuc, Douarnenez, and Plougastel. I found these names romantic and proud at the same time.

The brisk air of the ocean whipped my face and Marie-Reine's hair, like a crown of curls, which she took down in the evenings at the small hotels where we stayed. One evening on the beach, I watched her collect seashells during sunset. Her well-formed figure held me there like a magnet, paralyzed. Marie-Queen. The life I started was like an abrupt but delicious awakening to life. I saw the world in a multicolored prism. Moments spent with my sweetheart were like vacations in paradise.

I learned that Mary was divorced, but that she maintained a very good relationship with her ex-husband. When the Easter holiday arrived, we shared moments of real family life. I continued to study seriously because my success had to be proven in order to progress to other projects, but all the while

I thought, *she is mine, this wonderful woman is mine.* I felt waves of happiness rise to the rhythm of the tide. The future was limited only to being in her company and succeeding in my studies, although sometimes the question of my return to the United States plagued my thinking. For the moment, I did not want to imagine anything but the immediate days—our next romantic getaway, our next trip to Paris, and my next exam at the university.

Almost daily, Marie-Reine called to check on her son. When she called, sometimes I felt that something was upsetting her. "He is my ex," she said, "He is reluctant to let me talk to Jonathan at times. He doesn't like me disturbing him. But what does he expect? I'm away and want to hear from him."

I tried to reassure her and change her opinion, explaining that the child was on vacation, too, that she had to give him space to enjoy the presence of his father.

Some days, the calls dragged on with Franck, her ex, and she begged me to leave the room, so that she could solve her family problems. I felt a bit awkward, but grabbing a book, I went out on the balcony of the room to sit with the seagulls and listen to the snapping of the sails on the harbor. My love for her was so strong that I wanted to take care of all her troubles, but I did not want to intrude too much on her private life.

HOLIDAY PROJECTS

I made it a point to come back to New Jersey during the summer to settle a few things and to see my cousin, who was trying to get a visa so that our mothers could visit. It was difficult to tear myself from my lover's arms and leave her in Paris during the summer. I decided to make a big financial sacrifice and invite her to stay a few days in New Jersey. She told me that she dreamed of going to New Jersey. Nevertheless, it would not be easy to reconcile the stay with Mother Marguerite, who would be with us everywhere and whose interests would be different than my beautiful mulatto's. We would not have much privacy, especially if we all stayed at Justin's house.

This decision concerned me, so I had my cousin rent a small, furnished apartment for six months, the minimum the owner would give us, as an intermediate solution that would please everyone. I visited travel agencies to get tickets for Jonathan and his mother around the same date as my departure. I transferred a check and consulted my bank account, which began to decrease. However, I knew that my second-year scholarship was going to be paid in two months, so I could afford this unexpected expense. The savings I worked so hard to build served me well now and continued to grow.

I made a brief stop at the florist down the street to buy a bouquet of tulips for my fiancée and went to a bookstore to buy a comic book. Jonathan loved "Boule and Bill" because he dreamed of having a dog. I imagined a future not too far away: a white house in New Jersey style with a garden, and Jonathan's puppy, which looked like a big ball of hair, yapping in front of the house.

"Listen, little boy, I have a nice surprise for you!"

"What is it Benny?"

Jonathan nicknamed me Benny, which was easier to pronounce for him than Benjie. He snuggled against me, his face attentive and his eyes wide. I saw Marie-Reine, busy and smiling in the kitchen, preparing a *parmentier*, one of her little boy's favorite dishes.

"I'm taking you with me for the holidays. You'll see America."

"Bravo, bravo! Mom, too?"

"Of course. If she loves us, and if she is wise, she will come on vacation with us!"

"Mom, mom, did you hear that? We are going to America with Benny. I am going to see real Indians and cowboys, animals, bears, elk…!" Jonathan was shouting with joy and jumping up and down, clapping his hands.

Marie-Reine turned around at once. The smile that lit up her face a few minutes before suddenly dissipated. "What is this story? You know that it is not possible."

She addressed me in a tone of reproach, "Why did you say that to him? You know that Jonathan goes to his father's house for the holidays. Why make him believe impossible things? You are senseless; can you imagine his disappointment now?"

I was convinced that I made an unfortunate error and feared that the boy's tears would be my fault. I did not think he had to spend all his holidays in Martinique.

"I'm sorry, darling, I wasn't thinking," I said. "I booked you two tickets, but the date of return is open. We could stay a few days and then—"

That is it, and then he will leave alone as a big boy to the West Indies, of course. What? Do you want his father to declare war on me or what? When he leaves Roissy, I always know someone who goes home to have an eye on him, even if he goes to UM (as an unaccompanied minor). Anyway, I decided to go with her there to see my family too.

I saw big tears running down the child's cheeks, and he fled to his room, stifling heavy sobs.

"Well, you won. He will be inconsolable," she said. "I am sorry. I really wanted to please you. I did not think I could go on vacation and leave you both in Paris. I even rented an apartment for us."

"Look, Benjie, I did not ask you for anything. You did that without thinking. Anyway, before announcing this to the child, you should have told me."

I realized at that moment that Marie-Reine announced that she would also go to Martinique.

"And you, how long do you plan to stay? I thought you could not afford the plane ticket."

"Right. It is his father who buys the tickets to be sure to see his son. I think we will stay a month."

"His father? But he is unemployed!"

"He found work last month."

I felt a very bitter taste in my mouth, like bile, but with a taste of déjà vu, a repetition of a situation, and I felt very badly.

It was very difficult for us to get Jonathan to eat and return to a normal tone to talk to us during the meal and at bedtime. I decided not to stay in Drancy that night. I, too, was disappointed to have acted badly, and I was disappointed to learn that Marie-Reine hid this plan and that Franck paid for the tickets. I embraced the little boy, who, with eyes still red with tears, whispered in my ear, "Will I go with you one day, anyway?"

144

I dared not confirm it, fearing the wrath of his mother, but I said very low, "No doubt. One day when you are older."

The emotions of my departure to Maison-Laffitte were less passionate than usual, and my beloved did nothing to stop me. I did not persist, and with a heavy heart, I set off for the nearest metro.

When I let the door slam behind me at the bottom of the building, I noticed a big gray cat whose yellow eyes stared at me in the darkness. He did not even shudder at the sound of the closing door. Why did this cat catch my eye? I had, in a flash, the vision of a similar cat who, during our last romantic escapade in Brittany, took up residence on the corner of our terrace. He ran away one evening, scaring Marie-Reine who was leaning against the railing.

Tonight, I composed verses as sad as my heart, as if my soul as a poet lost all optimism.

Your magical look electrifies my body
It transforms hatred into a shroud of love
And trains me on its port
Where the nightingales play me their bad turns
My heart bleeds profusely
I love you, torch of my soul,

Let me to escape on the wings of a Flemish.

Do not make me shed tears

That make me hover in the delirium of ecstasy

Under your smile that crushes me.

                   - *The Tears of Love*, Lociano Benjamin

Over a few days, the storm dissipated, and I waited patiently for my queen to find her bright smile. I did not know how to approach the subject again with her. I would have loved to introduce her to my family, and to all of America!

I simply canceled the plane tickets and waited for my beloved to bring up the subject. I resumed my evening visits and our Sunday leisure. One evening, by chance, I heard a few snatches of conversation. Stealthily, as I watched TV in Marie-Reine's living room, I heard her talking to Franck. I first heard her mention the trip to Martinique, then laugh in a short, clenched manner. Suddenly changing tone, I heard numbers and exclamations. She must have been talking about money with him again. I focused on the TV show to avoid hearing any more.

Our nights resumed under the aegis of passion, sensual love, and erotic games. I did not tire of her body. Three weeks separated us from the great departure. I felt injured as she packed her luggage. Jonathan, perhaps told by his mother, no longer said anything to me and played quietly at night with his small cars in his room, no longer cuddling on my knees like in the past.

Then, the fateful date arrived. I booked my flight for the day before their departure so that I would not have to face the emotions of being alone at the airport. I preferred it to be the opposite, so I bid farewell at her door by asking her to call me as soon as possible, or if she was in any trouble. She hugged me tightly. "Do not worry. I love you. We will talk! Kiss your mother for me!"

I ran down the stairs without looking back, where a taxi was waiting for me. I almost fell on the threshold of the building when the cursed gray cat ran between my legs. It scared me, but he disappeared into the entrance with a hoarse meow. I glimpsed up at the balcony and saw the silhouette of my adored star dressed in the tight red dress that I liked, and the little hand of Jonathan, frantically waving. The taxi started like a whirlwind because we were late.

During the whole trip, I tried to control the emotions that gripped me. With my eyes closed, I waited patiently until the distance separating us from Roissy was covered in the beautiful bright sun that warmed Paris.

I knew it was not a sad departure or a break, but something felt dark and melancholy. I did not want to spend the summer away from Marie-Reine, but a little glimmer of joy danced deep in me. I also wanted to hug my mother and take care of her for three months. She deserved it.

RETURN TO NEW YORK WITH FAMILY

Happy who like Ulysses, made a beautiful trip
Or like that who conquered the fleece
And then returned full of use and reason
Living between his parents the rest of his age
  - Regrets, Sonnet XXXI, Joachim du Bellay

I often related to the ideology of Du Bellay, a French Renaissance poet whose work I discovered during my studies. I felt for Ulysses, returning to taste the joys of the family cradle after a series of fatal mishaps. By definition, my "little village" was only a facade, since I already opted for a powerful country that offered me opportunities to travel. My "return to the sources" was distorted. It was not in Port-au-Prince that my destiny was waiting for me now.

However, other convictions shook my thoughts. Should I settle in Paris to live there with the woman of my dreams? By refusing to accompany me on vacation, did she believe that we had no shared destiny because I would leave her to carry out my university career? Had she been more far-sighted and pragmatic than me in this matter? My heart was pounding with this painful questioning, so I decided not to communicate with her for the first few days of my arrival.

With open arms, sunglasses on his head, and a brown linen shirt and pair of light trousers, I noticed, just past TSA, my elegant cousin Justin advance toward me. I remembered the first time he greeted me in the same place, in the same way, a few years ago. So much has changed since then! I arrived with no resources, trembling with timidity, feeling exiled, sad, and vulnerable, but full of will to invest in myself and enter the sphere of intellectuals in this world of America. I realized my American Dream. My official language was English, my passport was American, my livelihood and financial support in my studies were American, and my way of life, too. I never denied my origins; I knew what I had in the country of Uncle Sam. Why on that day back home did I not feel as happy as I should have been? A part of me adopted Paris and was suffering from this separation.

"One being misses you and everything is depopulated." True, I came back alone like I had when I left almost two years before, but I discovered a treasure in Paris. She was the ideal woman. This mixed-race beauty was elegant, sensual, funny, who so many men dreamed of, no doubt. I knew she had feelings for me. She said the word "love" so many times, and we practically lived together. We shared our friends, our hobbies, our outings, and even our professional concerns. Trouble was looming on the horizon since her refusal to spend the holidays with me. I did not understand the nature of her relationship with Jonathan's father, and I sincerely feared that she decided to stay in Martinique on purpose, instead of accompanying me. These gloomy thoughts must absolutely be forgotten because I wanted to take full advantage of my return to New Jersey.

I planned to make a few visits to all the friends who supported me during my years of galley. I wanted to give a grand welcome to my mother and aunt when they arrived, completing the first and perhaps the last journey of their lives. Mother Marguerite had never left the island. I imagined her surprise, her wonder, her emotion, to hug me and to discover my new universe since the death of my father. I had not seen my relatives.

Justin spoke without stop and asked me a thousand questions about France, Parisians, my projects, and my university successes. He told me about the steps he carefully took to obtain a tourist visa for our mothers. I thanked him sincerely. I had not been very helpful in this area because he settled everything in advance.

We went to his new apartment. His business prospered, so he lived in a luxurious loft. I was glad to anticipate renting the apartment for me and my mother because my cousin no longer lived alone. I was welcomed by Belinda, who officially shared Justin's life. Belinda, whom I immediately called "cousin," was his secretary, but she quit her job to devote herself to married life and be a stay-at-home mother. Indeed, I saw her belly, which was just beginning to become round, and they confirmed that they were expecting a happy event at the end of the year.

"You will return in time to be the godfather! We do not have a godmother in sight yet, but we were waiting for you to bring us a good fairy," said Belinda.

At this evocation, I lost my footing and sat in front of a glass of good wine while waiting for dinner. I told them about my joys and my hopes, my disappointment and my expectations. I spoke for hours about Marie-Reine and Jonathan—our intense moments, our walks, our weekends in the countryside and in Brittany. I described our stay in Nice and the cultural emotions in Florence. Justin and Belinda approved, commented, and concluded that everything would be fine because things were moving very fast, which for them was a sign of fate in my favor. I felt wonderful in this family circle, and Justin suggested not to hold a prejudicial bitterness and to phone my fiancée tomorrow, assuring her that a trip to New Jersey, even if only for a few days, would be beneficial for our love.

I needed a little rest. It was late, and the next day I had to go take care of my new apartment, which was not far. Belinda had already gone to clean the apartment and prepare my bed, and she told me that she bought some groceries to start. She said I would like it because it was a pretty house, freshly repainted, overlooking a park, and in a very quiet neighborhood. I was so grateful to my caring family and accepted their hospitality until the next morning. The electricity and the telephone already installed would make this easier.

Emotion gripped me when I saw my mother get off the plane. She had a large colorful tote on her arm and was wearing a blue dress adorned with the twisted gold necklace that my father gifted her for their anniversary many years ago. His means finally allowed him to spoil his wife, the mother of his boys, with one of the rare prizes that she deserved. This emotion could not be contained for a long time. Marguerite's tears mingled with mine. I squeezed her tightly in my arms, which were at once tender, reassuring, and protective. Justin, too, in the arms of his mother, who was much older than my mother, tried to hide her tears.

Introducing the Big Apple to our respective mothers was no easy task. They looked up at the skyscrapers, breaking their necks trying to count the floors, and asked questions about everything. They looked at the urban fauna with a naive child astonishment and commented on everything they saw. Sometimes the circulation of cars in a hurry frightened them. Eager to fill their eyes with the spectacle of enticing and richly furnished windows, they were ecstatic about everything.

They looked at the police on horseback like an old acquaintance, an anachronism in this futuristic and delirious universe, but closer to the life they understood. The horses were reminiscent of their childhood, and they began to relive memories, telling Justin and I about picturesque characters, deceased ancestors, family history of past centuries, and family legends, which we knew little about. No doubt we were too young at the time to memorize the name of the great uncle of our mothers, Achille Destours. He had been with Jean-Jacques Dessaline, Henri Christophe, and Clairvaux, the young lieutenants of Toussaint Louverture, committed to the liberation of our country, and one of the heroes of the capitulation of the French in Vertières at the beginning of the nineteenth century.

They went on like inexhaustible griots. I heard names like that of the family of Dumontel, who I knew my mother and aunt were related to, and their family swarmed with voodoo priestesses. I heard more names that awoke some distant images of my childhood. An old lady with hair caught in a white cotton cap that came from far away to greet my parents. Mama Félicité was her name. One day she arrived with her adopted daughter who took her inheritance, Mama Calixte. I smiled at the memory of Mama Félicité. And yet, even before my father, there were many very distant events of this period of intense disturbances of the nineteenth century, as if these women had lived for more than hundred years. Were they not anachronisms in our lost society?

At that time, I was a kid more interested in playing outside and eating pastries prepared by my mother on this occasion. I know that Mama Félicité had a look that made me think of cat's eyes, a greenish yellow, and a hooked nose. Very weird for a mulatto. She had a sharp nose like that of a bird— an eagle—and an expression that grew stronger when she handed me a silver medallion with her long fingers like trees, telling me to wear it for protection always. This medallion represented the Virgin of Guadalupe on one side, and on the back were strange signs like a mystical prayer or magic formula. Her daughter, Mama Calixte, looked into the depths of my eyes for a long time and put her right hand on my head, as if for a blessing, then whispered something, approved by Mama Félicité's nods.

This memory became clear just as my mother was telling these stories, while just a few minutes before,

I would have been unable to remember anything about this! Suddenly, I realized that this medallion always accompanied me. I did not wear it around my neck, but it had been in the pocket of my wallet for years. Every time I changed out my wallet, I instinctively slipped it into the coin pocket, like an amulet. Nonetheless, without really lending faith to it, like a childhood memory or a worthless family jewel, I kept it by habit.

I went to get it and showed it to my mother, who said to me, "Keep this medal well, my son, it is your blessing and your protection because you are too vulnerable of a person. The distant relatives who gave you this knew that you would need it for your wanderings in the world, and because your heart is naive and too sincere. You risk dying of passion, without clairvoyance and judgment, when it comes to being abused by a woman. Love is your weak point. Be careful. My dear poet, when will you see the reality of the world?"

DREAM OF A SUMMER NIGHT

The name of one who has sworn to love all life
These moments of passion when love smiles at us
The time of a song that makes us shudder
It is a trip to the sun without risk of rain.
A breath that beats even stronger,
When we are face-to-face (...)
I cannot live without being near you.

- *Near You*, Lociano Benjamin

I was preoccupied for a few days, and the presence of my mother made the stay feel shorter.

The hours flew by in a whirlwind of activities: visits, reunions, shopping. I appreciated my old world, but with a state of mind that felt different than the one that reigned over my last months in New York before leaving for France. I dined with my old friend Mario who welcomed me like his prodigal son, especially in the company of my mother. I told dozens of stories about my life in Paris and my spontaneous trip to Italy. They never got tired of hearing about old Europe, with nostalgia for some, with envy for others.

On the advice of Justin, I finally dared to call Marie-Reine, but no one answered. I made two futile attempts. My mood darkened, but I didn't let it show. Her memory haunted my days and nights, and I began to imagine the worst. Maybe she did not want me anymore?

I felt obligated to tell my mother, who suspected something. She told me that she would always be my confidante, my privileged friend, even if I was no longer a little boy. She listened to the story of my lamentable divorce—betrayed love, bitterness, depression, even my desire to end my life—with great attention. I had hidden the details to spare her after her mourning. I saw tears piercing her eyelashes, but she did not break her silence and simply nodded her head to invite me to continue my story. I told her about the new opportunity that was granted by the university to study in Paris for two years. Mama Marguerite approved and took my hand when I told her about Marie-Reine, my queen who had refined elegance and overflowing sensuality.

She smiled and murmured, "Ah, Benjie, I only want your happiness, my child, but you always put yourself in difficult situations. You are too impatient and can only discern the passion. You should have waited to understand her situation before investing in this torrid bond that leaves you unhappy."

I tried to explain to my mother that I already imagined marrying Marie-Reine; but suddenly, I was invaded by uneasiness. I had not heard from her. Was that normal for someone who claimed to love you so much? Doubts about her relationship with Franck tortured me ruthlessly, and I made the decision to call her tomorrow, even if it took all day, to find out where we stood.

The night was very hot. I was thirsty, but a heavy tiredness prevented me from getting up. The murmurs of the street waking up came through my half-open window. I preferred outside air to the confined air-conditioned environments. My mother was sleep again. I was glad she could finally rest after so many years of hard work and suffering.

I heard a car slow down and a door slam. I got up to go take a look from the window and drink a glass of cold water. I glanced through the bay window to see a new yellow New York taxi turn at the end of the avenue. I didn't know whether I should read, make coffee, or go back to bed for a little while. Six o'clock rang at the neighborhood Baptist Church, where worshipers were preparing to attend the first service. A beautiful Sunday will rush families into the park or to cooler places nearby. Suddenly, I heard two discreet knocks at the door. Who was here? Justin, so early? Impossible.

Another light scratching. I was barefoot, the cool tiling gave me a pleasant feeling. I gently pulled the lock open, but I did not have time to register who was there. How was she here? How did her arms wrap around my neck and her mouth search for mine? How did we find ourselves entwined, clinging to each other like castaways?

I could not make a sound, and I lifted her back to my room, squeezing her as if she were going to escape. I closed the door and waved to her not to speak again. I wanted to take her in with my eyes. I caressed the silky fabric of her tight yellow dress and undid her black pumps with devotion. "*Tais-toi*, my love. I still want to stay in the world of dreams so that you do not escape." I spoke in the hollow of her ear and murmured crazy words. She answered only with a smile. It was better to enjoy this intense moment of emotion in silence, so I laid her gently on my crumpled sheets.

The minutes, the hours that followed were a perfect communion of our fevered bodies and impatient kisses. At times, I tried to tell her that my mother was sleeping next door, that she did not expect this visit either. It could wait, so I sank again into this abyss of happiness that she opened before me.

We awoke long after in the golden sun. I slowly regained consciousness; Marie-Reine was sleeping in my arms. A smell of coffee tickled my nostrils, and I lifted myself gently, worried like a teenager caught in the act, wondering if my mother was waiting for me. I stepped out of my room, and the sweet voice of Mother Marguerite came from the kitchen.

"Nothing like a good breakfast. Come, my son, you must be hungry." She went on, "I put the lady's bag in the closet and her vanity case in the bathroom. Such a pretty Croco bag!"

I was embarrassed, but my mom gave me her cheek that smelled like violet, as always, to say hello. "Shut up and eat. I do not need explanations."

INTIMATE CONVICTION

We were sitting on the terrace of a fashionable pub. I gazed with delight at the two young women conversing like old friends in front of me. Belinda, my cousin whose belly was still rounding, and my beautiful queen, with whom she laughed. They were shopping for the baby.

Justin savored his beer and exchanged glances of satisfaction with me. Our mothers, too, made purchases, choosing gifts of all kinds for family and loved ones back home. The only thing on my mind was my mom's next departure, because I suddenly wondered anxiously when I would see her again.

The relationship between Marie-Reine and Marguerite seemed warm, but a weird feeling gnawed at my heart. Marie-Reine did not really bond with my mother, whereas for me, these two women represented my strongest feelings. I felt that my mother was studying her, gauging her, without giving her absolute confidence. I did not ask any questions, and I drove any doubts out of my mind. I observed, however, that Marie-Reine was very generous with everyone. Nothing had a price tag for her, and I did not understand how she had so much money. She shopped lavishly at the shops on Fifth Avenue, which seemed beyond the reach of our purses.

Then came the day she told me she had to go back home. We had two weeks together. I did not know if I should return to Paris early, or stay a month longer than I planned; I wasn't supposed to return until October! "Tell me, honey, what do you want me to do?" I asked in vain.

She seemed indecisive. "I have to take care of some things, and even think about moving. You might be bored if you came back right away. Enjoy your family. I am very happy to have known this city, thanks to you!"

"But I can help you there, especially if you move. Did you find a place? You know I would like us to live together. We can try to find a bigger house for Jonathan and ourselves. I just need to inform Mr. and Mrs. Deaunier of my decision—"

I could not continue because she announced to me bluntly, styling her hair in front of the mirror with that sexy look I loved so much, "My darling, I will not have Jonathan this year. I decided to leave him with his father for a year because it was not easy for me. His grandparents want to see him grow up, and his father just opened a tourist agency. He has been working very hard for some time, and he is making a lot of money. I am going to send him a small allowance, and I will see him during the holidays. We agree now."

All this news hit me like a ton of bricks. What right did I have to protest, to give an opinion, to impose myself?

My mother quietly retired to her room. We were on the eve of her departure, and she finished packing her bags, feigning a cheerfulness she did not feel. I understood her sadness and tried to reassure her somehow. "No worries, my little mom, you see I'm living the life I've always wanted. I love Paris, and I'm doing well in my studies, I will come back to America ready to take a position that awaits me, and I found happiness."

Mother Marguerite shook her head in an enigmatic manner. "My child, my child, destiny is yours! What can I do?"

Everyone was in tears, and we did not stop embracing and promising each other to look after our health, to write, to call. Mother Marguerite told me that Paris was an inaccessible dream for many of my family and that I was lucky to return. However, I felt so much unspoken when her eyes fell on Marie-Reine, who was accompanying us to Kennedy Airport, and I did not feel very comfortable.

Then, arm-in-arm, the two cousins headed between laughter and tears to the terminal from where their plane would leave for Port-au-Prince. My heart sinking with deep sadness, I watched the majestic, proud silhouette of my mother fade away down the escalator to the runway. She turned one last time, and I noticed the mysterious look she gave Marie-Reine. I was convinced that my mother had a strong opinion about our future together, but I dared not confess that, in my opinion, it was far from optimistic.

FATAL REVELATION

We continue to hope for light, but here is darkness;
clarity but we walked in endless darkness. We continue
to fumble as we search for the wall, as blind people, and
we continue to fumble like those who are without eyes.
We stumbled in the middle of the afternoon like at dusk.
Among the vigorous men, we are like the dead.

- Isaiah, 59: 9,10

I already felt like a dead man, having paced
for so long in a world of endless darkness. After my
visit with *Mamoune*, I still hesitated to open my eyes,

still feeling myself prisoner of the darkness of this devouring passion.

Marie-Reine went, by work obligation, to Paris. She had the good grace to leave me a telephone message. When I called her back, she had to go. She was planning to return to All Saints for a few days. She asked me to excuse her because she had a lot of work to do, but she told me that she missed me and suggested that I free up my schedule to spend a few romantic days with her. All this was too much for me, but in my heart of hearts, the desire I had for her was most vivid. I promised myself that the next time I saw her, I would ask her to seriously focus on our relationship.

I waited for her in a little café in Montmartre, which I attended frequently before knowing her. The workers were friendly and discreet. I tried to focus my attention on the leaflets sent to me by a British university, where I intended to stay for three months to learn diplomacy. In my heart, it was my true ambition to become a diplomat. I obtained acceptance and a scholarship, as well as the prices for student housing, and I thought to leave in the spring after second semester exams.

I started to convince myself that I had to take time away from Paris. There were memories that haunted me, and I wanted to put distance between a bitter love that had a disastrous effect on me. I dared not believe that this moment of reunion would be beneficial for me.

Time passed very quickly and too slowly for my pleasure. The smell of coffee and chocolate floated in the air. A florist set up a stall on the pavement opposite, and the pots of fall-colored chrysanthemums made me think of my father whose grave would be well-bloomed and cleaned, blanched with lime in memory of the deceased. I think of his tall figure dressed in white check trousers, his soft smile, and the fabulous stories of his young adventures in Cuba. I looked through the slightly misty window. Father, do you see your son from up there? Do you also feel his distress and his malaise? I am not the way that you raised me, dad. I wish nothing more than to be worthy of you, even if I am no longer in your image. What would you say, dad, if you were here? I tried to remember his low and serious voice, slowing lighting his pipe while sitting on the terrace enjoying the evening coolness. Melancholy invaded me!

Who was this? Two cool hands landed on my eyes, but I had not seen anyone coming. It could not be her! I put my hands on hers, sliding her fingers to my lips before turning around. Radiant, she threw herself around my neck. The reunions between us were always amazing, but, unfortunately, distorted my sense of understanding.

She wore a magnificent black woolen coat, supple leather boots rising up to her knees, and a short black skirt. Her face emerged from a red turtleneck, and she had cut her hair at the shoulders. I searched her painted eyes and her greedy mouth. I wanted her, but as a desperate soul who wanted what he could not have. I now saw, with a sharper and more critical spirit, her expensive clothes. I smelled her perfume. It was a new fragrance of amber; one that I did not recognize.

"My love, finally! I missed you so much!" She said.

She settled in front of me, taking off her coat and fluffing her hair with a nonchalant gesture. On her wrist shone a heavy, gold bracelet with charms that I did not recognize either. I was once again crossed by a thousand contrary thoughts. Did I believe them?

Power of love
Whose kindness arises
Like a bodiless monster...
Sadness beautiful face.

I talked in platitudes—about the sticky weather, my project in Nottingham. She tilted her head, her mischievous look on me, but sometimes glanced to the old-fashioned decor. She looked for the contact of my hand on the table. I did not know, once again, where we stood.

"Where are we going?" She murmured greedily.
"Before dinner, I will do good things to you."
"To your home, no?"

Her eyes turned away, and she looked confused. "No, I cannot go there. I have almost nothing. There's no heat since I left. I had the electricity cut off."

Should I act surprised to force her further into the lie? I did not want to hurt her. A remnant of love forbade me.

"Come on, I know a little hotel not far from here. We will see after."

The hotel was covered in pastel fabric. The tiny window opened into a courtyard with two potted shrubs that had seen better days.

"Turn left. Room 24. Take the elevator down." The receptionist, leaning over his newspaper, barely looked at us.

I followed her down the stairs and barely opened the door before she smashed against me for a languorous kiss. I lost my mind. I embraced her, and as in New York, a flood of passion threw us on the bed. I undressed her, pretending to discover her beautiful bracelet. "Oh, what a beautiful jewel! I've never seen it before."

"I bought it in Italy."
"Ah, you went to Italy. I did not know."
"But that's not important, come on."
I persisted, "It must be expensive! I would have gone to Italy with you if you asked me."
"Darling, what is wrong with you? We are in the middle of something! Are you going to blame me for fleeing the confined world of my lab?"
"Do you love me?" I asked the fatal question.
"You see that I am here. I love to make love with you."

"I know, but I am asking you if you really love me. I am not talking about sex. You know my feelings."

"Be quiet, you're confusing me. I wanted to have a good time with you, but you ruin everything!"

The bewilderment on my face was obvious. I felt a gaping wound open in me.

"Come on, Benjie. Please, stop torturing yourself, I beg you," she said.

The evening seemed very short, but I managed to stay calm and save my questions for later. She gave herself to me freely. She stayed with me all night, and we barely found time to take a short break and nibble some food in a small café nearby. For a few hours, I focused on our past good times, her laughter, her deep voice, and her greedy hands when they embraced me.

We went for a walk, hand-in-hand, but returned to the hotel because the humidity was unpleasant. I asked her about Jonathan and details of her work in Switzerland. I asked how long she planned to stay there ("Another month or two to be successful in her new job," she claimed); her relationships there ("super nice colleagues," she said). She told me about a potential romantic encounter and laughed uncomfortably. She defended herself saying, "Life is so full of risks, and opportunities are short. I always come back to you, you see!"

Here, I understood. Although jealousy and disappointment gripped my heart, I found the strength to hide my pain this time. I acted as if I heard nothing. I answered in a flat tone, "You're right, you should never get tied down. You have to live. By the way, did I tell you that I'm leaving Paris around March?"

"Ah! Where are you going?"
"I can join an introductory course in political science in Nottingham. It's a course for foreigners in the School of American and Canadian Studies."
"You won't even be in London? I love shopping in London!"
"If you want to see me, you can come to the university. It's two hours from the capital!"
"It is not the same!" She sighed, biting a fingernail delicately and stretching like a cat who just woke up.
"Marie, it's time we have a serious discussion about us. If this is not going anywhere, please tell me."

"I have nothing to say that you do not already know. I love you! I spend wonderful moments with you, but I do not want to live your lifestyle. I do not want to spend all these years, when I am still so young, calculating expenses and budgeting while you are still getting your bearings. To your credit, you are great in school, but, my dear, you are far from starting a career. I love luxury and freedom. I am sorry. We've been together a long time, but you're not the one I want to be with forever. I want to live, to be drunk on champagne, make love, buy designer dresses and jewelry, and travel in first class. My salary is not enough, and your student funds and your five-or-six-thousand dollars in savings will not work for me. Sorry, honey, really! You wanted me to talk, so I did. I prefer to be honest with you, but if you wish, we can still see each other here and there. I really like being with you. You make me feel good, you know."

Her cynicism twisted my heart. I did not want to hear any more. *Mamoune* warned me, and Josselin also knew from Leah about her true intentions. Suddenly, my star died out.

WHEN THE SUMMER ENDS

(...) I remember another year
It was the dawn of an April evening
I sang my beloved joy
Sung love in a manly voice
At the moment of love of the year.

- *Alcohols*, Guillaume Apollinaire

The drizzle that blurred the park gave a weeping look to the trees in the garden that I could see through the misted window. My return to Paris plunged me into a heavy sadness for two weeks. Michele Deaunier was very caring and attentive, but did not know how to make me smile again. I resumed my classes and spent most of my time with modern novels or symbolist poets. I spent a lot of time on my presentations and notes.

The gloomy weather in the autumn did not encourage me to go out, and I did not want to hang out in the bistros with my friends, who respected my desire for loneliness. The professor of modern literature was very demanding, but his passion for writing pleased me, and I wanted to get excellent grades in the class. However, my heavy heart remained deeply ill at not seeing the object of its flame again. Indeed, Marie-Reine announced to me by telephone that she had to go to Zurich and Geneva for work. These trips would be more and more frequent this year for her and all her colleagues. I did not know when she would return. I felt abandoned.

My meeting with my her was very brief, but for two hours, we exhausted our vital forces in a hot embrace. The interior of her home was bare and cold because she had packed up most of her belongings, telling me that she sold some furniture in the living room and dining room. Only her room and the kitchen still looked like I remembered. I did not dare enter Jonathan's room to see what was left. The absence of the child, to whom I was really attached, upset me. She confirmed that she wanted to move to a studio or two-room apartment, since her son was still in Martinique. This surprised me, but once again, I dared not ask too many questions, respecting her decisions.

Yet the same anxieties haunted me. What was the point? For now, I did not have a diploma that would fix my situation and offer her something concrete. She would not marry a simple student. I realized that my feelings actually made me lose my sense of reality. I wanted to test her love so that I was certain there was nothing between us except carnal passion, behind which were no lasting feelings. Paris in grisaille did not make me dream anymore.

The month of October seemed endless. Gusts of bad wind and rain cleared the parks of Maison-Laffitte and brought out umbrellas. I always arrived soaked to the bone at my destination, whether at university or home. The metro was crowded with people more than usual, hats and coats dripped on your legs during the trip. I preferred to borrow books from the university library rather than work on-site like before. I could not wait to get to my studio and stuff myself with hot coffee from a café, waiting for the phone to ring in case my queen called me.

To top it off, I caught a horrible cold that kept me in my house for three days, where I pitifully absorbed the teas and broths Michele prepared for me. Fortunately, I did not miss important classes. If I could, I would have jumped on a train or plane bound for Switzerland, but I did not have the strength. I waited.

I did not hear from her until the following week—in the form of a postcard showing snowy mountains. I learned that she went on a hike with colleagues over the weekend when I was waiting for her call. Dismayed, my heart hurting, I seized a book at random and plunged myself into the poetry, which always dressed my wounds and relieved my troubles.

I read verses of Apollinaire in the collection of *Alcohols Marizibill*:

I know people of all kinds
They do not equal their destinies
Undecided like dead leaves
Their eyes are fires out of their hearts
Their hearts move like their doors

I lingered on the poem titled Mary, of course:

The masks are silent
And the music is so far away
It seems to come from heaven
Yes, I want to love you, but you hardly love
And my pain is delicious.
When will you come back, Marie?

I passed the bank of the Seine
An old book under the arm
The river is like my pain
It flows and does not dry
When so will end the week?

My Dear Son,

I am still thinking about the wonderful journey you allowed me to accomplish. It was an experience that will brighten my memories, and that I will tell my grandchildren. As you suspect, all our family, friends, neighbors, and even your former teachers, were waiting for me to give them news of you and tell them about America. Aunt Agathe and I have told a thousand details over and over again. We are all proud of you, of your success, and what you still have to accomplish, with the grace of Our Lord. Aunt Agathe was also delighted by Justin's success and eagerly awaits the birth of the baby so she can come back and spend some time with her daughter-in-law, whom she loved so much. Belinda is so charming, so cute.

However, my son, I did not come back as happy as I would have liked because I'm worried about you. I fear that you will have your heart broken. I see that you have not changed; you are still the passionate young man who, unfortunately, is blind and helpless when he falls in love. I guess that is your destiny. However, a mother cannot see her children suffer, and I pray that God will come to your aid and help you see clearly.

I saw our great cousin, Calixte, and I told her about my fears, asking if she could help you. She told me that you are not at the end of your troubles. The spirits visited her, and she prayed for you. Keep the medallion safe that she gave you when you were a child. According to her, you were born under a bad star with regard to love and women, although life otherwise will always smile on you in terms of studies and the career path you have chosen. She also assured me that you would eventually find your wife, but after a long road paved with pitfalls, deceptions, and betrayals.

My child, I do not know if I am guilty of doing something that marked your destiny of sorrow. Nevertheless, Madame Calixte revealed to me that you *were unceasingly under her protection without knowing it. Continue to pray and restore your future to the mercy of the Lord. I do not want to slander the young woman that you presented to us; but, in my opinion, she is not worthy of the love that you give her, even if you are physically attracted to each other. I have the impression that you are her toy. She has other ambitions, and her spending scares me. Think carefully, my boy!*

With love and kisses,

Your Mom.

I kept reading the letter that I just received from Port-au-Prince, and I was stunned by it. My mother had never told me so clearly what she thought of the girls I loved, leaving me free to decide. She warned me about my vulnerability and naivety as a dreamy poet, but never criticized the woman I loved or the woman I married. I understood that her impression of Marie-Reine must have been disastrous, and I tried to remember why she seemed displeased. Of course, there was her reckless purchases, her whims, the fact that she left me without news for several days; and especially, the mysterious situation surrounding her husband. My mother measured all this by the yardstick of her love for me, but how could she blame Mary? She only wanted my happiness, but here I was waiting around with blind trust. But, for how much longer?

I wanted to evolve into a normal relationship, but I realized there was nothing normal about what I was going through. I remembered the words that Josselin told me when he accompanied me to Roissy some months ago: "It's unstable in everything." Who could enlighten me and help me now? My friends were temporarily unavailable. I did not want to worry Michele with these stories. Who could I tell? My only interlocutor usually was my notebook of poems, but today, I needed concrete answers. Paul Eluard wrote a text that fit like a glove, and I learned it by heart:

Barely Disfigured

Farewell sadness
Hello sadness
You are inscribed in the lines of the ceiling
You are inscribed in the eyes I love
You are not quite misery
Because the poorest lips denounce you
By a smile Hello sadness
Love of the kind bodies
Power of love Whose kindness arises
Like a bodiless monster

185

Disappointed head
Sadness beautiful face.
And I cried,
I cried in front of my candid simplicity,
Then I laughed at myself.
Sadness was my lot for too long,
And misunderstanding too, madness, uncertainty, spite,
leniency, generosity, frustration. I smiled Because I
decided to take the bull by the horns and react.

It occurred to me that I must see *Mamoune*, Marie-Reine's old friend from Martinique. She was a wise woman, with a Creole accent I loved, who we would visit sometimes. She seemed to be a frank and direct person. I wanted to contact my beloved before her return to give her one last chance to convince me. I had several phone numbers of hotels where she stayed in Switzerland. I hoped she was not in a meeting or at work with her cell phone off. She had to answer my call because I did not want to be forced to record a message on an anonymous mailbox.

Too bad for me. Her phone rang once, twice, then three times. At the end of the fourth, the sweet voice of Marie-Reine explained that she was not reachable and blah-blah-blah... I left a brief message: "Saturday. The little bistro in Montmartre where we ate with your son. I will be there at five o'clock. Kisses."

FUNERAL OF PASSION

How did I find the strength not to sink into the madness of despair during the week that we spent together? I worked during the day and saw her in the evenings, sometimes quite late. She spent most of the time shopping. We had drinks at the café, spent time at a hotel, and I accompanied her to the RER where she left to go to *Mamoune*'s home, who was hosting her. I did not suggest that she stay at her apartment.

I endured. She waited for me one afternoon after my classes at La Sorbonne. We went for a walk in the Luxembourg garden, like before. I held her hand, but we no longer exchanged languid kisses as in the past, ones that cut us off from the world and reality. We enjoyed light conversation, without forcing intimacy, like old tired lovers. I could not bring myself to burn the bridge. I was weak and sensitive. I lashed myself inside for still feeling hope. I did not want to think about what she did to me, so brutally. I operated in a state close to amnesia, not to mention with total anesthesia. I waited for her to leave without apprehension and much less impatience, with a kind of cold indifference.

In the old, lonely, and frozen park,
Two forms passed.
Their eyes were dead, their lips were soft,
And we hardly heard their words.

In the old, lonely, and frozen park,
Two specters evoked the past.

Do you remember our old ecstasy?
Why do you want her to remember?

Does your heart still beat my name alone?
Do you always see my soul in a dream? -No.

(...) And the night alone heard their words.

                 - *Sentimental Symposium*, Paul Verlaine

The level of incomprehension that hit me made me feel dumb. She was indifferent to anything that was not a carnal relationship. Her departure was almost a relief. Too much misunderstanding and doubts tarnished my feelings. I wanted nothing more than to take refuge in work, in my books.

I began to write feverishly during long winter evenings. I was intoxicated with poetry. I let it flow from me, taking shape on the white page, forming my sorrows and my joys. My uncertainties and my discoveries merged into one character: the beloved woman who I still loved. The poems eventually constituted a collection, which I called *Tears of Love.*

In a dreamlike state, I proposed the manuscript to the *Universal Thought* in Paris. I was incredulous that my literary success was so easy. Poetry saved me. Marie-Reine was the catalyst that allowed me to realize my ambition. In just a few months...

I lived these moments in a mixture of happiness and enthusiasm. My friends celebrated this first success, and the Deauniers held a dinner in my honor. I was overwhelmed with work. I fulfilled all that I imagined, and always in love with love. I no longer lived a misadventure that left me bloodless, another joke of fate. I did not give up or stop the process. I felt, unlike what I experienced during my unfortunate experience with my wife, combative and relentless to one day find the woman who was waiting for me.

It was with great joy that I left Paris to go to England and devoted myself thoroughly to this introductory course in diplomacy. My future seemed to finally open on a road paved with satisfaction and gratitude.

EPILOGUE

So, Al-Mitra says: Tell us about love.
He raised his head and looked at the crowd on which a
great silence had fallen.
In a confident voice, he says:
When love beckons you, follow him although his paths are
steep and arduous.
When he wraps you with his wings, yield to him.
Even if the sword hidden in his penises hurts you
And when he speaks to you, believe in him.
Even if his voice breaks your dreams like the devastating
north wind.
If love crowns you, it crucifies you too ... (...)
Love does not have and cannot be possessed because
Love is enough for love.

- Of Love, Khalil Gibran

I was crowned and crucified by love, hurt by an invisible sword, but now I felt grown up and wanted to reach my goals. It was in this second state that I fully enjoyed the progress of my studies and accumulating knowledge. The days passed without trouble, and I felt confident in better days.

Yet, one day, I received a message on my answering machine that troubled me. Josselin said, "Come as soon as you can. Marie needs you."

I took the first Eurostar the next morning. My heart was alert and my nerves tensed. A few hours later, I got out of a taxi in front of the apartment of the one I continued to love despite everything.

Unusual commotion reigned in front of the house. I saw Josselin speaking, using big gestures, with two men in gray suits. One of them held his briefcase like a clipboard and scribbled on a piece of paper. I saw people place boxes, an armchair, and paintings I knew well onto the sidewalk—the Haitian paintings that decorated Marie-Reine's living room. I passed almost unnoticed in this whirlwind. I heard a high-pitched cry that I recognized as Mary's voice, who cursed as she emerged from the building. She tried to grab one of the imperturbable men, disheveled and furious. She screamed without shame or restraint. Neighbors appeared behind their curtains and on their balconies. I was petrified and had no idea what was going on. Josselin, who finally noticed me, rushed toward me wildly.

"Finally, you are here. She is being evicted." On the sidewalk were books, a stereo, and two suitcases of Louis Vuitton. The two large men continued to grow the heap.

Marie-Reine saw me, too, and rushed toward me. "Benjie, finally, darling, do something."

I did not tighten my arms around her when she hugged my chest. I felt like I was watching a bad movie. The weather was mild, yet I felt cold. Passersby starred at the clueless and agitated group that we made up. I perceived a sneer on the lips of a young person who lit a cigarette while watching us.

Between sobs, she told me that she was being evicted. The rest of her belongings had been seized, and she only had left what was spread out in front of the door.

I felt neither pity nor sorrow, but suddenly shame. I immediately recalled her inconsiderate purchases, her carelessness. I contemplated with almost disgust her Hermes bag that she held tightly against her. Josselin, the faithful friend, tried to gather suitcases, boxes, a basket of soft leather shoes from Italy, and other assorted items.

I hated this moment and wanted to go underground, make myself invisible to the curious, prying neighbors. She firmly handed me a document to sign. At first, I refused. In an icy voice, I ordered her, "Sign that. We're leaving." Then I told Josselin to call a taxi. I wanted to get out of this nightmare as soon as possible. Josselin replied that he had his car, but not everything would fit in his trunk.

"Call a taxi. I am telling you, please!" I tried to keep a normal tone, but I did not recognize myself, so cold, so detached. Marie was still trying to grab the lapel of my jacket. I pushed back slowly. "Calm down. There's nothing you can do right now. Go to *Mamoune*'s house."

She wiped her eyes and put on Christian Dior sunglasses. All this luxury and vanity repelled me. Did she need all this? She was beautiful without these artifices and priceless accessories. She was a materialistic woman who wanted to live beyond her means. Had she not done enough? I thought about Jonathan and gave thanks to heaven that the child did not have to suffer through this—safe at his father's house. The bailiffs asked her for the keys to her apartment. She pulled them from her bag and dangled them in their face. A queen who draped herself in false dignity. Finally, I pitied the woman who I had idolized and loved so much.

The taxi parked in front of the house, and we somehow loaded the luggage. Josselin took the paintings and boxes and waited for my orders. I gave him *Mamoune*'s address, and then rushed into the car where Marie-Reine was already fixing her lipstick. So much frivolity made me angry. "Dammit, explain yourself."

She tried to rub against me, but I pushed her away.

"I want to know how this happened," I said.

"Well, I could not pay the rent, what do you think? I had to pay for the hotels in Switzerland. I intended to take care of it, but I did not have time. I was looking for another apartment, you know."

Her bad faith drove waves of adrenaline through my body.

"Well, I will drop you off at *Mamoune's.*"

"But I have nothing. You proposed before that we could live together. I thought..."

I did not want to hear any more. "That was before. I changed my mind. I have too many things to do, and I decided to return to the United States at the end of the school year. I gave you your chance. I gave you all my love. It's over. I have suffered too much."

She sobbed, but I did not want her to soften me anymore. No doubt, I still had an old feeling of attachment to the one I wanted to be my wife, but shame and disappointment made me strong and lucid. I had only one desire: to leave her and never see her again.

"Do you have money?" I asked.

"Almost nothing."

I took out my checkbook and wrote a check for two-thousand euros. It were as if I were buying my freedom. A new life without her for a derisory sum. Freedom had no price.

"Goodbye, Marie-Reine." I wished her good luck.

Your love crowned me, but you crucified me. Kiss your little one from me. May this bad moment serve as a lesson. You should learn to live more modestly and be more responsible, more stable. Damage for you, a pity for me—for us—but it is no longer possible, you understand. *Adieu.*

LEAVING WITH MY HEAD UP

I can write the saddest verses tonight.
To think that I do not have her. Regret having lost her.

Hear the immense night, and more immense without her.
The verse falls in the soul like dew in the grass.

What does it matter that my love could not restrain her?
The night is full of stars; she is not with me;

That is all. In the distance, we sing. It is far away.
In addition, my soul is unhappy because I lost it. (...)

I do not like it anymore, it is true. Yet how much I loved
her

- Pablo Neruda

The party was in full swing at Maison-Laffitte. My hosts organized a big barbecue in my honor. The month of July reared all its heat. With the new century, the climate felt disrupted. There was talk of future heat waves and the dangers of global warming. This warm evening was the culmination of all my successes, and my evening of goodbye to all my friends who were invited for the occasion. Josselin and Champs joked and called me *"Maître"* or *"Monsieur l'Ambassadeur,"* with amused reverences. Good humor dominated this pleasant hubbub. I felt nostalgic about leaving Paris and its lights, but also its traps, and its foolishness. I recollected, between two glasses of champagne, the memories, as they danced in my foggy spirit. My friends and colleagues gave me worried glances from time to time, because I never knew how to hide my feelings. Josselin inquired two or three times, "Are you all right, Benjie?"

"Yes, I'm OK. Do not worry. I am leaving, but you will see me soon here or there. My friends, I owe you so much."

I thought that the wheel of fortune again changed course. I had so many new experiences. I refused to let myself feel any sorrow whatsoever. I was convinced that new adventures were opening up to me, and I counted on the new century to finally find my place, my way, and my stability.

Moreover, I had to leave those invaluable friendships that supported me so well in difficult times. Tonight, they were all there with me. I was the object of their attentions, their warm complicity. I had to go out with my head up, full of gratitude for these people from so many different backgrounds that I would hold forever in my heart.

A job was already waiting for me in New Jersey. I wondered if I should move back there, since there were old demons there that still bugged me. I thought of a little town, Roselle, which I appreciated for its calmness, its discreet shops, and its provincial charm, not far from New York.

As always, I counted on my cousin to prospect before my arrival. According to him, I would find decent housing in my budget. My savings were practically exhausted, but I could count on my salary as a teacher come September.

I wasn't shy to contact schools and universities for work. Montclair State University offered me an interview with the dean of the French department. I knew that my CV suited them and that I had a good chance of being entrusted with a class or two of students in French language and literature.

One of my great joys was to see once again my talent as a poet rewarded. I won the poetry prize of the Academic Institute of Paris, and I imagined myself as a poet and diplomat in the future. Why, then, dwell on a painful past, that could have undermined my will and my appetite for study? Once again, I left without regrets and without looking back.

I now had degrees from the Sorbonne, a certificate of training at the University of Nottingham in Diplomatic Sciences, a prize for poetry, and a collection of poems. These tears of love produced literary successes and renown as a poet.

On the other hand, I came back with a part of myself that felt abandoned by the torments of an unfortunate passion. I knew that, despite my good resolutions, I would not soon forget the sting.
However, in the strength of my age, I felt like a tiger hungry for fame and recognition in my country.

It was a great pleasure to teach curious teenagers the language that I loved, and to share my innate taste for beautiful works. I taught the history of words, writings of French philosophers, and rational thought. I was so far removed from the subjective expression and the poetic dimension of the feelings, which for that very reason I constituted an admirable teacher worthy of the greatest respect. Ah! Make them share my passionate taste for poetry!

MISS CITRONNELLE

The winter winds chased the dead leaves, and hard months passed. I found myself surrounded by my old friends, my cousins, and especially my new colleagues. I spent hours correcting papers, preparing my classes, and documenting my thesis. I moved into a completely renovated apartment not far from my office. I invested more time than probably reasonable in the courses. I delivered a lecture of my own research to my students.

On Sunday's, I went to the local church to pray with the congregation and sing in the choir. I met so many simple and good people. Then, I went for a walk to run some errands while listening to the radio—always a Haitian station.

From time to time, I went to my cousin's house to relax and share the Sunday meal. My little goddess, Serena, would jump on my lap, filling me with love. I tried not to think of having children of my own. Solitude was my bitter companion, but it did not make me unhappy. The wounds of my sacrificed heart had not quite healed. Even at work, I was no longer interested in female colleagues or in any other women that came my way. I gave my sympathy to Literacy.

I worked with a doctor of letters, who graduated from the University of Nice. He was from Africa and contracted to teach French for two years at Montclair State University. His wife, a teacher too, followed him. They filled me with quality conversation, and we had rewarding exchanges. I sympathized with their situation because their children were scattered between Rwanda and France and had not been allowed to come with them. They hoped with all their might to be able to reunite their family shortly. Their culture stimulated me and pushed me to deepen my own knowledge.

It felt like time was passing slowly, without a hitch, making my life feel smooth and satisfying after so many tumults. I was invited to the calm and reviving home of my cousins for Thanksgiving. I found that little Serena looked more and more like her mother: so pretty, fresh, and adorable. Justin finally found his stride, and that made me happy for him. That day would come for me, too.

From time to time, I looked at the strange talisman that was always in my wallet, and I wondered if it would hurt me or protect me from now on, because it already tested me so much. Was I armored against the torments of love? Had I suffered enough because of women? I knew that my poet's heart was recovering, but I remained forever "the poet with the broken heart." From time to time, I wrote poems again, but on more varied themes about my island or Africa, the origin of our roots.

During the Christmas holiday, I wandered through the illuminated city of New York. The attractions and fake Santas taking pictures at crowded stores made me nostalgic for the Christmas from my old life—in the beautiful surroundings of Provence under blue skies with my friends. I missed them, and telephoned them from time to time when I was in France, England, and Port-au-Prince—from

English to French to Creole with such sweet pleasure. "Merry Christmas, Merry Christmas." Peace on earth and good will toward men. My road was paved, I no longer feared the hazardous future. My work was enough for me, and the few people I met I kept close.

Why, after months of my benevolent routine, did I have the idea to see my old friends at my old boss' garage? I found myself face to face with my old friend Mat on a beautiful spring day. He was working on a superb Italian-brand convertible while talking, always, with a cup of coffee in his hand. He exclaimed, "Benjie, what are you doing here?"

"Mat, what a surprise! I just stopped by to say hello. What have you been doing?" We greeted each other warmly.

One by one, we recounted our mutual adventures during the last three years, because I had not seen Mat since my divorce. He himself was always seductive and mysterious in the eyes of women. He had broken up with his partner and was once again the single womanizer I had always known.

"I found you, old man, and I will not let you go! You have experienced many problems, but we will heal everything," he said.

His joy was sincere, but I explained to him that I did not go out much and that I have been a loner since my return.

"Nevermind. That will change. I have two tickets for an event next week. I was planning to invite a young Brazilian I met last week, but she can wait. You must come with me. You need to get out a little!"

His warm enthusiasm was infectious, and I agreed to accompany him the following week to the Citronella Ball, a beauty pageant.

"You will see so many beauties! In the end, it is better that I do not take my Brazilian because we will have plenty of women to admire! Who knows? Maybe we will be lucky," he added maliciously.

He laughed and little charming wrinkles stretched around his eyes. He had not changed, and I thought an outing would be good for me.

"OK, then. I am in. If we dance, I admit I am a little rusty. I feel like I have not danced for centuries!"

We exchanged numbers and made plans for the following Saturday. Mat would pick me up at my place. "Listen, to fit in, you must wear a shirt or tie in shades of green of yellow," he advised me.

Love is a child of bohemia He has never known a law if you do not love me, I love you and if I love you, take care of yourself...

This passage from Bizet's *Carmen* haunted me. I did not know why, because I never had a particular fondness for *bel canto* or operetta. Everything I knew was taught to me years before when I worked at Mario's with Clara. I listened to the repertoire of singers of the sixties and seventies, who seemed to express feelings in simple and poignant words, I loved Charles Aznavour, Jacques Brel, Claude Francis, Daniel Guichard, Jean Ferrat, Adamo, and Christophe. I loved American crooners like Sinatra and Dean Martin, and Cuban or Latino songs.

A little wind of madness crept into my head, and I realized that I was looking forward to going out. I was happy to see my old friend Mat again. I should find the time to buy a new tie. This thought pleased me because since my return from Paris, I had not bought anything new. I had enough suits that I brought back from Paris.

The evocation of Paris and its department stores made my heart ache a little, and I felt again the pain that I negated for so long. I strove to change the course of my thoughts and to drive away the ghost Marie-Reine, whom I never heard from again.

WONDER

I carefully chose a lime green suit and a pale, yellow shirt. I perfumed myself with Christian Dior's *Eau Sauvage*. The fragrance diffused its halo of buried memories that threatened to reappear. However, I shielded myself. I was going to have a good evening; have fun and laugh with my old buddy. Curiously, I no longer thought about Ariane, and I was grateful to my friend for not even mentioning her name during our last conversation. After a last look in the mirror, I thought I looked elegant and ready to make the most of the evening.

The room was already crowded and resonated with indistinct voices. An old blues song played, but it did not fully cover the noise. Mat was also very elegant in his dark blue suit, green almond shirt, and a green-and-navy-striped tie. He bobbed softly between the tables, looking for our seats, already attracting the eyes of women in long dresses of light muslin. I saw them all, but could not distinguish any in the hubbub, busy following the wake of Mat.

"Ah, here we are! Apparently, we will have company because it is a table of six," exclaimed my friend. He added with a laugh, "I hope we will not have old barbarians or frightened virgins next to us all night."

I laughed in response and accepted the chair he presented me. "Stay here. I'll get a drink while we wait," he said.

I ordered a glass of champagne and waited for his return, finally taking in the people around us. I noticed with pleasure that many of the young women were dressed in charming green and yellow and wore a badge with a number on their bodice.

I understood that they were potential "misses" and began to gauge them out of the corner of my eye. Some seemed relaxed and laughed heartily. Others looked more intimidated or worried, touching up a curl of their skillfully-arranged hairstyle and smoothing their skirts. Others sipped colored cocktails and casted glances at their competition. There were chatty and silent, young and old, very thin and others more plump. I devoured their eyes without hiding my curiosity and admiration.

Mat came back with our drinks, making his way through the crowd. The music changed to a furious boogie tune that made the guests stomp their feet and shake their heads and shoulders.

"There are some beautiful ones, right?"

"They are all sublime. Thank you, at the very least, for the company and the show," I told Mat, who had eyes only for a chiseled blonde-haired woman in a flowy dress. "I see you have chosen your prey," I said, laughing.

There was an announcement at the microphone and people all headed to their tables. A woman sat down next to Mat, almost in front of me, and I felt a stab in my heart. She pretended not to see me and urged another young woman to sit next to her. Then, an older woman took a seat at my side. I stood up to present the chair and she accepted with a forced smile. I noticed immediately, despite the differences in ages of each, that they must be family. The second young woman stared at me immediately with shameless eyes and an engaging smile. "Good evening, gentlemen!" She said.

Her eyes went from Mat to me, probably wondering who her date for the evening would be. The other barely looked at us. Her head turned slightly toward the runway, she waved at a man in his thirties who seemed to be looking for them. He joined our group and extended his hand to greet us, "Mike Desroches!"

"Hi, Mike." I am Mat and this is my friend Benjie." Mat shook his hand, and I did the same.

"Nice to meet you," he said, "This is my mother, Ada, and my sisters, Luce (he pointed to the youngest who held my hand too long) and Eva."

The mother and Eva briefly nodded to me and began to talk about the show that awaited us, the election of Miss Citronelle. I realized that the two young women were candidates. I stealthily admired the imperial profile of Eva, her perfect body molded in a yellow satin sheath, which highlighted her cinnamon complexion, long golden nails, and almond eyes. Her full lips were colored in a pearly, brown shine. Her sophisticated hairstyle, made up of multiple ringlets, was rolled in a bun with a golden fishnet. She was the most beautiful woman of the evening. Her shimmering eyes were neither green nor brown, but dotted with specks of gold.

Her sister, Luce, more graceful and playful, was also a beautiful and fresh beauty. In her green and yellow frills, she seemed extinguished next to her neighbor.

Mat started a conversation with Mike, and they seemed to get along. After some mundane words, the mother and daughter began to speak Haitian Creole, and my heart began to beat faster because I finally saw an opportunity to attract their attention by speaking to them in our language. The ice was broken, and Eva seemed to relax a little. I wanted to enter her field of vision because she seemed to ignore me from the beginning.

She wore the number one on her generously low-cut top, and I did not doubt for a moment that she won the first prize, even if the one that attracted Mat at the start had every chance to win because her beauty took everyone's breath away. I knew that Mat only came out with exceptional women, but overall, Eva had an unusual personality and a magnetic charisma. To me, her beauty absolutely eclipsed all the candidates. She had a melodious voice and a laugh that made her perfect teeth sparkle. Her gazelle eyes had a velvety depth.

Luce, however, received more advances and smiles. She looked like a young leopard hunting. Her very bright eyes promised passion, and she opened her lips by sticking out the tip of her pink tongue every time our eyes met, to the point of embarrassing me at times. Her attitude was a call, a game of perpetual seduction, intended either for my friend or for me, while Eva seemed sure of her enigmatic power without even blinking.

The show was magnificent, and the meal was succulent. Between the shows on stage, the contestants danced with elegance and care, as not to mess up the fancy suits of their dates or their hairstyles before they presented on stage.

As I expected, Eva was sublime and unbeatable. She answered with humor and a lot of spirit to the trick questions posed to her by the host dressed in canary yellow.

"Who is your ideal man?"

"The one I have not yet met."

"How do you envision your future?"

"Wearing Eve's outfit with Adam."

The spectators applauded and whistled. The rounds followed one another, and Eva was invited to dance on the dance floor. She was asked for the name of her partner, and to my amazement, she walked over to me and took me by the hand. "It's him," she said.

I suddenly found myself under the fire of hundreds of looks, intimidated and flattered at the same time, and panicked at the idea of looking clumsy. I did not know what we were going to dance, and I was relieved to hear the first notes of a waltz, which I knew. I was caught in the middle of an enthusiastic audience and the feeling of a flexible and firm body in my arms. The surprise would have nailed me to the ground if I did not have this obligation to help her defend her title.

"Why did you choose me? I thought you didn't care. I am flattered, but I am afraid of—"

"Shut up," she answered in a breath.

Concentrate. It is as if you do not know anything about women. Her sudden familiarity and her tone of contempt made me strong, so I replied, "So hang on, we will burn the floor, and you will win."

Tilting her head back, she gave me a defiant look. That evening, I became the date of the one who had no trouble winning first prize and the crown of Miss Citronelle.

Her younger sister, second runner-up in the end, coached Mat on the dance floor, as well. My friend saw his dream of the Scandinavian blonde disintegrate before his eyes, because the lady, first runner-up, proved very attached to a man of about fifty. He wore gold rings and chains, smoked a big Havana cigar, and smelled of money and smugness for miles. Mat, meanwhile, responded to Luce's obvious advances. I thought they would end the evening together, at least the few hours left before the morning.

I escorted Eva until the end of the night. I had the pleasure of seeing her triumphant look when she let her shimmering eyes run over the room where the conversations were trying to dominate the deafening music. The beauty lacked modesty, but her beauty, which I studied attentively, continued to delight me. I found her perfect, and the votes of the public confirmed my choice. I was proud to have contributed to her win.

At one moment, I caught a fleeting glance from my friend, and I had the impression that he was envious of me, and that Luce was his worst enemy. She was now ignoring him royally as if being beaten by her sister had chilled their relationship. I could not decipher the thoughts of the mother, who had eyes only for her daughters, especially for the oldest who she seemed to venerate. I understood after some reflection that the true head of the family was Eva. That did not matter to me. I had only one idea in mind — to find myself alone with her; to break the magnetic shell where she was shut up in an ivory tower, a deterrent dungeon placed above all others.

See a world in a grain of sand and a paradise in a wild flower. Hold the infinite in the hollow of your hand and eternity in the present hour.

\- William Blake

I was done for, here again in the trap of love as a prisoner, a consenting victim. My heart panicked, blood beat in my temples, and a shiver ran down my back from time to time when her golden green eyes settled on me like an indecisive butterfly. *I do not want her, I do not want her,* but these were empty words because each fiber of my body craved her.

Her long, golden nails teared my heart as they touched my chest, and her wildflower poisonous perfume was not paradise, but a hell in which I wanted to delve with delight. I would like to live in her embalmed wake, hold her forever in the palm of my hand. I was nothing to her, except a grain of sand in a vastness, which frightened me. She whirled in my arms to the sound of the music, as expert in dance as she was in seduction. I was captivated, and I shuddered every time I took her hand to twirl her and bring her back into place. I felt like she was tearing my heart out with her feigned indifference.

Yet, I was glad to see she refused all the men who dared approach her, except Mat, who got up before me for a languid slow dance to Sinatra. I was scared then, and for the first time, too, jealous of my friend because it only took one look for women to swoon in front of him. While he swayed on the floor with Eva, I thought to make him jealous with Luce, but that thought seemed so ridiculous.

Very quickly I realized I was wrong. Luce stuck to me, and after two minutes, I was convinced that she was interested in me. Her fingers stroked my neck and caressed my back and shoulders. If it were not for fear of causing a scandal, I would take her out on the floor. I turned so that I had a line of vision to the dozens of couples on the floor. Eva in the arms of Mat. I noted with a sick satisfaction that she did not surrender more with him than with me, and I was relieved to still have a chance.

I smelled the potent perfume that revealed her presence near me. She invited me without a word, with a simple nod, to a new dance. She must have felt my emotion, but acted as if she were an inaccessible and sovereign goddess who did not understand. I feared the worst, but threw my entire self into this spiral that engulfed me. Nothing else existed around us. I could not even hold a conversation. I said everything through my silence full of fervor and passion. In my trembling arms and shaky breath, she said nothing either. She made me her toy, her slave, her thing. I am yours, princess, I am yours, mistress, I am yours, my beauty, my poison, my wildflower, my beauty, take me, I am yours.

ON MY LIFE

On my life, I swore to you one day
To love you until the end of my days...

           - Charles Aznavour

Mat, who against all odds left alone without Luce, was not talkative, evading an answer when I told him the plans we made with the Desroches family next weekend.

"I do not know. I have to take care of my Brazilian," he said. "I do not feel those two girls, nor the brother. They were like parasites attached to the older sister, like the others."

"You think?"

"Of course. I talked to him while you were making sweet eyes at the Miss. He wants to do business, but without scale. He speaks a lot, but does nothing. Luce is a sexual animal, in spite of her youthful air. Frankly, they do not interest me more than that. Be careful, my friend, you are blind, as usual. You will be vaporized by this family, and the beautiful Eva is a manipulator. She will put you under her spell, and you—I know you—you will dive in headfirst."

I was a child by my friend's assertions. My reasoning was fuzzy, and I could not balance things rationally. "I think I fell in love. I am in love."

Mat burst out laughing. "As if we couldn't tell! You will never change. Have you not had enough problems with women? Be like me. Seduce them, feel good, offer a small gift, a weekend in the countryside, and then *ciao*, goodbye, *adios*. Women, Benjie, are less complicated than Eva. They just want to go out and have fun, too. There are few who dream at our age of a single, traditional love; a life centered on a husband, children, and a home."

He added after a moment's reflection, "Besides, did you know that your beauty already has a twelve-year-old daughter?"

I remained quiet. I danced all night with her, but I did not know anything about Miss Citronelle, whom I already loved without limits.

"I talked with the brother and the mother, and Luce is talkative," he continued. "You were too busy staring at Miss Eva like a dead fish to have asked her anything. Poor innocent poet, I should have warned you, but I also should tell you that this woman has a shop, a hairdressing and beauty institute two blocks from your house. You will see for yourself that they are two man-eaters. If you had money or social status, you could interest her for a while, by the way of a miracle."

The words of my friend resounded painfully in my head and despaired me. Before closing the door in front of my apartment, Mat added, "Believe me, give up! If you want, I will take you to meet other girls who are less complicated. Next time, we will have a good time. Go on, sleep well and forget the fate this bad fairy put on you."

I returned, completely disoriented and severely pained, trying under an icy shower to restore order to my mind. However, when I put my shirt in the laundry and hung my suit on its hanger to air it out, a smell rose to my nostrils. Eva's perfume was there, stubborn, like an evil charm to weaken and invade my life, my apartment, and my thoughts. Ah, Estée Lauder, I thought, inhaling deeply. A sexy and magical perfume like her!

I slept very badly that night and waited until the next morning to decide my destiny. Was I going to follow my heart, or follow the path of reason, as my friend advised? Contradictory thoughts ensnared. I believed that Mat was envious and disappointed that he didn't find someone that night, so he tried to leave with his head up. He did acknowledge his own failure. Yet, he could have reluctantly seduced the young Luce, who looked like a hungry wolf in search of human flesh and was not shy toward men.

However, Eva, Eva, I wanted her for me. The fact she had a twelve-year-old daughter did not bother me. I loved children! She must have gotten pregnant at sixteen or seventeen, so I was only more inclined to pity her and help her. Deceivers (I thought of Mat and his unscrupulous life as a Don Juan) disappointed many wonderful girls. Eva must have been a victim of life and men. I wanted to show her that we could be serious and responsible people. I decided to call her that evening and ask to see her again, not with her family, but alone, and confess my admiration. I hoped with all my heart that she would go out with me and get to know me, trust me. The fact that she was able to provide for herself and her family with her business only made her more valuable and deserving. I blamed normal mistrust for finding herself in her situation.

The day passed, and I was feverish, undecided about how to approach Eva on the phone. What if she hangs up on me? I would go the next day to her studio. It was on Main Street near my home. I would find it easily, being normally ignorant of this detail. I would introduce myself as a client to have my hair cut. I would pretend to be surprised at the coincidence, so as not to frighten her. After imagining many meeting scenarios (like if I waited for her at the door of her institute with a rose, or if I surprised her when she came home), I was still uncertain, so I decided to drive quickly by without knowing how to get there, so that the meeting seemed fortuitous and not premeditated.

When destiny was decided, we could not change anything. A small white dog with a black-stained chest suddenly appeared under the wheels of my car, while I was distracted passing in front of Eva's workplace. The building displayed in Gothic black letters "Studio EVA." I braked suddenly, but the sound of barking made me expect the worst. People turned around or came outside to see what happened. Suddenly appearing from the corner of the street was an angry Luce, frowning, who literally threw herself on me, "Look what you did, driver!" Then, recognizing me, "Benjie, is that you? What happened? You crushed the neighbor's dog! What are you doing here?" She leaned against me, almost clinging indecently to me.

I was stunned under the double shock of surprise and embarrassment. I explained to her that I lived nearby and that I had gone out for a drive. I did not know what to say to her. I would have fled at full speed if I could. It turned out that the dog had been more afraid than hurt. I felt bad.

Luce took me by the arm and said, "Park your car here. We live in the house at the corner of the avenue. Come have a drink, you do not look good at all. But, I am so happy to see you again."

I could not put my thoughts back in order. I told myself at one point that I met my goal without mounting an elaborate meeting from scratch. I was going to see Eva again, to enter her house, and afterward, I would confess. Unfortunately, I was disappointed when I saw that Luce was the only person to welcome me in the house. She insisted on giving me a drink and cuddling against me, under the pretext of comforting me. She caressed my head while I drank a large glass of sparkling water.

I tried to free myself. "Listen, Luce, I would like to see Eva. Tell me about her. When is she going to come back?"

"Forget Eva, honey, I am here for you." Luce tried to kiss me by pressing her body against mine. She had an expert talent, it was true. I almost forgot myself because I was so confused. She was thin and molded in a white dress that was very short and unveiled long legs sitting on the couch near me. Her hand began to explore an intimate part of my anatomy, when I pushed back forcefully. I would have given in if I had not been so obsessed with Eva's face. I was a young and fiery man who had been without love for many months. She quickly understood my excitement and tried to take advantage of the situation. However, as it was a purely physical reaction on my part, I was able to control my feelings.

"Stop, I do not want to go further. I would like to see your sister. I have to talk to her."

"Eva! Eva! Why, what do you want with Eva? I am not good enough for you? Poor idiot, my sister will dump you like that! She will break your heart! You will not be first or last! She will take advantage of you, and she will throw you away like an old Kleenex. She will destroy you, idiot! She will take advantage of you because you are neither rich nor good enough to make her yours. You will come back to throw yourself at my feet so that I console you. I swear, it is going to be like this. You are wrong to deny me."

She was mad with anger, and her eyes sparkled with fury. She began to cry at once, changing her tone, "It is unfair. I had feelings for you as soon as I saw you. I felt a great attraction. I just want to be loved, get married, live as a couple, have children, but I only have the moldy crumbs that Eva leaves me. You will do as others do. You will suffer, and you will realize too late that I am more sincere."

I got up to leave, barely saying goodbye, leaving her to her cries and tears. I went out of the house like a crazy haggard, not knowing how to escape the situation, and returned to my car. The white dog was sitting in front of the car, licking its dusty legs. Realizing that it was the cause of all my misfortunes, I kicked him, "Go get, dirty."

He escaped yapping as before, but I met his yellow eyes that did not resent me, and I felt very sad and angry with myself because I did not like to be violent toward animals. I immediately regretted my actions and started in a hurry to hide.

EVA!

Eva! Who are you? Do you know your nature well?
Do you know where your goal and your duty are?
Do you know that, to punish man, his creature,
To have put his hand on the tree of knowledge,
God allowed that above all, love of oneself
At any time, at any age, he did his supreme good,
Tormented to love himself, tormented to see himself?

But God so close to you wanted you, O woman!
Delicate companion! Eva! Do you know why?
It is so that he looks at the mirror of another soul,
That he hears a song that comes only from you:

Pure enthusiasm in a sweet voice.

It is so that you are his judge and his slave

And reigns over his life by living under his law.

Your word of joy has despotic words;

Your eyes are so powerful, your appearance is so strong,

That the kings of the East have said in your canticles

Your fearsome look equal to death...

- Les Destinées, Gérard de Nerval

Very disturbed by the scene that Luce inflicted, I spent horrible hours rehearsing these words, re-reading this poem only because the name of my new star was written there. Eva, the first of all, and the last (I thought). Never again would I love so intensely. My heart was worn out by so many withered loves that it threw its last strength into this battle. Despite the misadventure I just experienced, despite the fear that Eva's sister now despised me and I did not know what she could do to harm me, I did not want to let go. I had to face this unforeseen difficulty, to do everything to attract Eva and muzzle Luce. I feared her reactions as a scorned woman. If I were not in love with Eva, would I have fallen into her web? What if Eva came in at that moment? I did not dare imagine what could have happened.

I held out for three days without calling, while at every moment I was burning to dial her number or go to her shop. I was absent-mindedly lecturing, eyes lost beyond the lawns of the campus through the large, open windows. The summer was approaching, and the days lengthened. At other times, I would have taken refuge in my office or at the university library as soon as classes were over, but I was only concerned about meeting the one who consumed me with silence. I still needed to prepare the exams for the students, to answer their anxious questions. I was sorry I did not spend all my time with them like before. I ran away from my colleagues and shaved the walls like a thief. Love causes reactions that are so incoherent, so irrational. It should be a source of joy and inspiration for the poet, a muse for the painter and the musician, but for me, it generated feelings of guilt and anguish.

One Thursday, I went out to buy some ink cartridges and get some groceries because there was nothing left in the house. I headed to the store, and I knew that my steps would lead me inevitably to a small building topped with a sign of Gothic letters that indicated Studio EVA. The mere idea of seeing her name written on the facade excited me already. I may have the chance to see her emerge from behind the window, looking astonished to see her and invite her to have a drink before she went home. I hoped with all my soul that she would be alone. Anyway, I would need to do it before Saturday because I had plans with the whole family that day. I blamed myself because I could not imagine facing Luce again. I felt guilty that I did not do anything. I preferred to find myself only in the presence of Eva and send all the others to hell.

I walked slowly along the sidewalk, hands in my pockets. I stopped at the corner of the street, watching the light shine through the window behind a white Venetian blind that was half lowered. A customer came out of the studio. She had her hair, nails, and makeup done. She smelled like hairspray and beauty products. Nonchalantly, I headed for the door of the building, and she was in front of me, wearing tight jeans and a white bustier that raised her chest. She held a bunch of keys in her hand and was headed to the drugstore. This was an opportunity because I think I forgot something on my shopping list.

I entered after her into the shop and found myself in front of her in the magazine department. When her shining, astonished eyes rested on me, I think I melted on the spot. It took her a few seconds to identify me, and then she smiled deliciously.

"Hey, my escort! What are you doing here?" She offered me her cheek and I kissed it, trembling.

No more excuses or evasions. I answered her, "I was waiting for you."

"You did not call!" She retorted. "We have plans to go out on Saturday."

"Let's go for a drink. It is not too late, and you worked all day!"

"You know when it comes to going out, I am always down!"

The ice was broken. I must now give my all to woo her. And just like that, I found myself in front of the blank page of a new chapter of my life.

We had a drink and exchanged a few pleasantries. The hours passed like a blip, so we went to dinner. She warned her family that she was not coming back. I devoured her with looks, and I found that she felt good with me. She laughed, told anecdotes, and talked about her daughter as if I had known her for a long time. She talked about the burden on her. She took care of the family, but her business was good. Having brought her family over from Haiti just a few years earlier, she knew that her mother could only count on her because Luce and Mike worked only irregularly. The father of her daughter, whom she never married, sent her subsidies from time to time and took the kid for the holidays. She loved cooking, traveling, going out, and dancing, but was quite secretive about her private life. She departed from her first coldness, and her charm stirred me.

The night was very late when I brought her home. I did not know if I should kiss her or not, but she did not let me hesitate long and approached me with her luscious lips. She told me, "See you tomorrow! Come and pick me up at my work around nine."

What happiness, what emotion. I reconciled myself to the existence and blessed the god of love who touched us with his grace.

The way back was star-studded, and life was smiling again. I exulted and began to plan our evening tomorrow, which would be the prelude to a revival, a turning point in my life. I must not be too impatient, realizing that the initiative should come from her, but I did not care. I was already enslaved to the new mistress of my heart. She had character, but under the impassible layer of her hardness. I understood that she was a woman full of resources, willpower, courage, strength... the qualities I missed.

I felt a comforting power emanate from her. She dominated me, and I only wanted to be her slave.

After this evening, things rushed at a pace that made me drunk and prevented me from thinking. The evenings followed each other, and we had family dinners here and there. We shared little moments of intimacy at the bar on the avenue that separated our homes. We finally became more sensual, more physical. My beautiful Eva accepted an invitation at the end of those swirling weeks to spend a whole night at my place. We began to share our little habits, to share the wardrobe and the bathroom shelf. Her favorite tea found its place near my coffee bag. Her snacks were in the kitchen cupboards, and in my room, sometimes a pair of silky stockings were languid on a chair near the bed.

I went to her house for dinner sometimes at the end of the week. Ada prepared a meal for us. I laughed with Eva's daughter, Ingrid, a curious young girl with bright eyes were so similar to those of her mother and her aunt. She adopted me as a friend, a confidant. She made me listen to her music, and sometimes I asked for help grading homework while Eva got dressed to go out.

I avoided being alone in the presence of Luce,

who looked almost hateful when her eyes were on me or when her sister and I left, arm-in-arm, to go to a show or party with friends. On Sunday's, we went to church together, and she joined the choir to sing with me. Pastor Amédée liked to have me sing solo, and in these deep moments I sang only for Eva, closing my eyes sometimes to hide my nervousness from the congregation. She knew that my voice rose for her from the altar where we were sitting near the choir.

I could not count the weeks and months that passed like a whirlwind of strong feelings, outings, music, and Sunday evenings watching television at home. I did not really want to spend my evenings with the women of the family. I found them a little boring because the conversations were about women who did not fascinate me, memories of their past that I largely ignored, or gossip about people I did not know.

But I almost shared the daily life of this extraordinarily beautiful woman, who was so close and so inaccessible in appearance. I avoided being too tender or eager in front of the family. I was modest in my actions because Ada reminded me of my mother, and the presence of Luce or the young teenager inspired me with restraint. I devoured my beautiful Eva, caressing her hand from time to time or placing my arm on her shoulders when we were sitting side by side.

"I feel like you like my daughter, boy!" Ada told me, giving me a gentle pat on the head. "More than you know," I answered. The others laughed loudly at my obvious trouble.

Mike made regular appearances in the apartment to drink and eat with us. He pulled his sister aside before leaving, and seeing his satisfied smile as he buried his wallet in his pocket, I realized he was asking for money. Eva never refused.

Finally, this *modus vivendi* began to weigh on me, and I began to consider moving in with Eva. I did not know how to announce this decision, or how to convince her to leave her dwelling. This would simplify our life, allowing me to adjust my schedule because my workload had shifted. I worked very late, and after our dates, papers accumulated on my desk. I could not find the time to read or write. This love devoured me.

Her final test, the father of her child, traveled a lot, but would come by from time to time, to my chagrin. Eva politely dismissed me, claiming that he was still very jealous, and, not wishing to argue in front of the child, she preferred that I not be there. She was sullen before the visits, but very lustful after, as if to reward me when he was gone. However, it was the only nights I could totally devote to my work.

I noticed that old Ada bent over backwards to prepare dishes for her pseudo-son-in-law, and I also felt some jealousy. It was then that the idea of living with Eva took a more concrete form in my head, but I could not calmly settle the budget we would need to get married. Still, I became more impatient every day and made the decision to tell her about this idea as soon as I found a larger house. However, I still refused the idea of living with the mother, the occasional brother, and the capricious sister, pouting and envious of my relationship with Eva. The young teenage, did not bother me. She was attached to her mother and certainly did not bother a soul, so she would accept this situation without worry.

I was surprised one evening, after we had spent a few hours of passionate love, to hear her say, "Honey, we have to do something. We cannot go on like this."

With a beating heart, I asked her, standing up on one elbow, my head resting on my hand, "Explain, I'm listening." I carelessly continued to caress her with my other hand, sliding my fingers on the smooth skin of her shapely legs.

She told me calmly, "You should get us a house. I will keep my apartment, it can be used, and above all, you have to keep growing up in society. You told me you started studying to be a diplomat, well, know that I would love to be the wife of an ambassador or a consul. Just imagine, we would travel, we would receive important people, and I would throw parties. I would dress at the Italian or French couturiers. I would put Ingrid in a posh college."

I did not know what to answer because I had not thought that far ahead. "That is why you want us to live together?"

She laughed, "You do not catch flies with vinegar," she said, jumping up and heading to the bathroom. "You have the merchandise in hand, it's up to you to pay. I'm not going to stay in a banal relationship for years."

A small bell of alarm rang in my brain, still mistaken by the pleasure that we just shared.

"Banal, you hurt me by saying that. My relationship with you does not seem trivial to me. Eva, I love you, I only ask to live with you, but under what conditions? For the moment, I cannot devote myself to another job. I must continue to collect my teacher's salary. I need it to ensure the future. If we have to move—"

"I will only move if my new life suits me!"

I was speechless because I did not know what to think, what to believe. I suddenly had doubts about her attachment and feelings toward me. I learned, at my expense, to be wary of the ambitions of women and their desire for luxury, and I was a little annoyed to pass for a "banal relationship."

Eva announced to me, as if to torture me more, "By the way, I cannot see you tomorrow. I have to leave for the rest of the week. I have to go to a black beauty salon in Atlanta; anyway, you work, the time will pass fast, but think about what I told you. I do not want to disappoint my family!"

She left me thus, without me being able to react. Had she chosen to go out with me to lead a brighter, more exciting life? What else could I offer her in the next two or three years? It seemed the nightmare that I already experienced was coming back to life to terrorize me. No, Eva, not you! Yet, doubt began to make its way into my confused brain.

I could not sleep that night, scaffolding a thousand scenarios of our lives, arrangements with the family, and the time it would take to find real estate agencies and move. The time of daydreams probably lasted long enough. You have to take your destiny into your own hands and assume the life of two (or three, or how many?)

I could not imagine that I could put all this family under the same roof, support Mike's regular visits, but most importantly, live with the one I accused of being a threatening snake, Luce. It was impossible for me to think that I could forget her attempt at seduction. I was suspicious of her and could not stand her secret meetings with Eva very much either. She often pulled her aside to talk "girls," as she said, but they willingly lingered outside with a thousand excuses, while I waited with Ada or Ingrid, helping clear the table, cook, or finish homework. Of course, these tasks in themselves were not unpleasant, but they were routine, family, our daily life. I had the impression that this was the unsurprising pattern of married life, after the emotions of the honeymoon.

When the two sisters finally returned to the fold, accomplices, laughing, I wondered what my role in this relationship was. At times, I gazed at Eva from afar and found her so elusive, so strange. Sometimes I felt her gaze on me, and I burned myself into thinking that I had an extraordinary woman that everyone envied. Finally, I also realized that this relationship was gradually cutting me off from my family, the few people I visited before, because I was so absorbed.

The family outings on Sunday's included worship service, a visit to the pastry chef and the florist, and lunch at home or in a friendly neighborhood restaurant. We went from time to time to play roulette at the casino, not that the games were my cup of tea, but because the trio of Desroches women loved the thrill of playing for hours. "Black, odd and go; red, missed, nothing goes; I double my bet. Do you still have chips? This time it is good. It is rigged. I will try again. Be cute, go get me a drink."

All this tired me. I played about fifty dollars, then made myself the knight by serving these ladies, my darling too busy forcing her luck at the game. I detected unknown glimmers in her eyes as if the gold flakes they contained became more intense and even more disturbed. I was always attentive and patient. The important thing for me was to be able to touch the object of my flame and my demon.

How to describe the days during that time? They are confused in my memory. I cannot see her between two clouds, being pushed by the breeze. I do not see her bent over me. I do not see her gentle gestures, fragrant hair falling on her shoulders, silky robes, or half-tinted, mysterious smile when I took her hand during our frequent outings.

She told me how excited she was to see me. She watched my steps when, my work finished, I returned to the room where she was waiting for me, immersed in the reading of her women's magazines, lying on my bed. We extinguished the lamp, and we whispered our love in secret.

She was quite different when we were alone, getting rid of her haughty pout to give herself to me. However, the next hour, her coldness worried me. She was suddenly absent, not sharing her thoughts, and if I questioned her, she raised her eyebrows as if to say to me, "What are you looking at?" What a strange relationship!

I could not say anything against her sister, who was always distant and contemptuous of me, because she bitterly defended herself. Oh, if you only knew, my love, how Luce's presence made me feel uncomfortable, especially since the day when Eva was supposed to be home late. She said to me with a bad look, "Poor idiot, take advantage of this moment of grace because with my sister, it will not last! Trust me!"

I did not even want to know what she meant by that, and when I saw Eva feel so far away, I remembered those nasty words.

Life was quiet for a few months, when one evening the phone woke me. It was Luce. "Go to the Domino, my sister is there!"

"What is happening? Is there a problem? I was asleep!"

She began to sneer at the receiver, and this incident disturbed me to the point that I jumped in jeans and a polo and found myself, a few minutes later, driving my car, on the road that led to the "Domino," a cabaret in view of Park Avenue. I did not see Eva that night because I had too much work, and she told me that she wanted to rest, too. What was happening?

The room was smoky and Cuban music played. There were potted cacti in the lobby, a carved wooden bar, and fisherman nets for décor, which gave this cabaret a falsely tropical look. Discreet booths housed barely visible couples under dim lights. Fortunately, I put on nice shoes and took a jacket in the process. Otherwise, I could not get into this discreet meeting place. I found myself feeling stupid immediately. What was I doing here? I must leave quickly. I must look like a madman, barely awake, inquisitive eyes. What was I trying to find, to prove?

I went to the bar and accustomed my eyes to the darkness. I observed the couples sitting in these recesses, delimited by iron wrought gates and hidden by palm trees and other green plants that hid their faces. An affable waiter came to me. Will I be eating at the bar? I had to order, so I chose a tropical and colorful cocktail. He brought it to me quickly, and I tried to guess the faces of the customers through the grids. I was tired and alert at the same time because I wanted to know. What was Eva doing here? Maybe she just decided to spend some time with a friend or to relax away from her family. However, she did not tell me anything. Why was Luce not with her? I do not know where she called me from. Maybe she wanted to play a bad trick on me and keep me from sleeping. I felt really silly that she made me come. I will swallow my drink and leave as fast as possible. I gave twenty dollars to the waiter, and while he collected my change, I turned to the opposite side of the room.

There she was with her back turned, which explained why she had not seen me. The young man who held her hand looked very young, like a Don Juan *gominé*, with his shirt open against a muscular torso. She was wearing the cheetah print dress that I loved. Her curly hair fell back into an asymmetrical mass on her bare shoulder. I did not see his face, but the charming smile of her companion made me realize that he told her some sweet spoken words, and she must not be insensitive because she leaned more toward him and put her second hand below the table. He planted a kiss on the fingers that were stretched toward him. He laughed, and she laughed with him. That excited him, and he bent to talk to her more closely. He perspired desire, and his eyes focused on the face of my girl.

I did not even react. I looked like this scene did not concern me, because I could not look at this whimsical picture and believe it was not me. It was as if the order of universal things was suddenly abolished, as if I lived a nightmare from which I wanted to detach myself.

"Sir, sir, your change," the waiter looked at me curiously, "Are you OK?"

"Yes, it is nothing! Thank you."

I wanted to leave very quietly without being noticed, and go back to my place and back to sleep. I got up very slowly, but I felt that my legs would not carry me. *Get out of here, get out, what are you waiting for?* I tore myself off the counter and went through the door, and the warm night filled my lungs and the music faded behind me. The door closed on the vessel where my love was frozen behind plans of adultery.

Adultery? We were not married, just lived together like eternal fiancés. I understood then that if I did not do something, I would lose it. Curiously, I could not get angry or blame her. I must be "banal," as she once said. Yes, I disappointed her. That's it. I'm insipid, too predictable in my doctoral routine: university, copies, research for my thesis. I understood that all this weighed down a woman who wants to rely on an active and responsible companion. I lacked passion, and everything was my fault. Yes, everything was my fault. *Mea culpa.* I knew she was waiting for a commitment on my part, and I hesitated for reasons that I could not get over. I loved Eva, but I did not like her family! She was the one I wanted to make happy, not Luce or even Ada, who finally disgusted me because I saw her game clearly. She attracted men to her daughters by her courtesy, false sympathy, good food, and her fake complicity. In addition, her parasite brother. Ah, I hated him. Nevertheless, I was the one who misled; I was in the wrong.

AN OLD FRIEND

Life resumed its routine course from my small apartment near Montclair, where I was entrusted with second year classes in French language and literature. I took on a few extra hours at a high school in the same neighborhood. I let myself go between my busy days and the few meals that my cousins invited me to share on Sunday or Saturday night. I went out a little, corrected papers, shopped for essentials, read, and sometimes daydreamed. I listening to a Haitian radio that I left on continuously at home. I furnished the apartment with the bare

251

necessities, having no time to run to the stores to find the superfluous. I was fine, far from the hustle and bustle of the latest events that once again made the implacable wheel of my destiny turn.

At the beginning of my forties, I found myself devoted to my professional duties, but also plunged back into research to write a thesis about my country, Haiti. I worried from time to time about my misanthropy and isolation, and I had a hard time convincing others that I felt OK. Once again, I was recovering emotionally. I left France as a sleepwalker, bruised once again and still desirous of rebuilding my existence at home, among the people who were my landmarks in my adopted homeland. I committed to a destiny that reached out to me to become a teacher. I was proud of this obligation. Why seek further happiness while what I had was enough for now?

LUCE

After folding the bag of Kraft paper where she buried the doll made by Mama Calixte, Luce fled, almost stammering. The ceremony impressed her, and she felt contact with the supernatural beyond what humans could conceive. She felt fear and satisfaction to finally have her vengeance!

The acrid fumes that the old witch filled her box with gave her a headache. She ran through the uninviting streets of this poor neighborhood of Port-au-Prince, where she may have a bad meeting. The dilapidated hovels followed each other, identical in their misery. She sometimes ran into a stray dog, which she avoided looking at, and a frightened hen flew almost under her feet. Awkwardly, she uttered a little cry of fright. She did not know how this animal rose under her feet.

Poorly-formed little gardens and messy little courtyards stood next to each other. Old tires and rusty bicycle frames bloomed behind the rattling palisades. Not a soul was alive at this hour besides dogs and wolves. Only silent shadows seemed to haunt these dwellings with closed shutters. She, who was accustomed to the colorful animation and the hectic life of the Haitian cities, wondered about the unusual place that seemed to be a different world from the one she crossed in the afternoon.

She felt like someone was following her. She turned around worried, and realized that she was carrying the misfortune in that bag of brown paper that hung at the end of her arm, which suddenly horrified her. However, her hatred was stronger than anything else, and she pressed even harder for the slightly better lit avenues where she would find life, normality, and taxis that would take her back to the upper town, sheltered, on land she knew.

She lingered on this young pretentious girl who would soon be disillusioned. Why had he preferred her? Luce was consumed with jealousy since that day when both of them, hoping to be elected Miss Citronelle of the year, dressed up in their finery to go to the contest. She spotted first this tall, elegant young man, who at once occupied the entire space of her heart and that she desired almost painfully. It was love at first sight, yet he only had eyes for Eva, her older sister, already the mother of a teenager.

Eva always got the men she wanted. She was more mysterious, cold in appearance, and she looked at men haughtily. She devoured males with an ogress appetite. She was demanding in everything, and they ate out of the palm of her hand. Luce only had the remains from her sister, and had to play the considerate sister-in-law, the confidant. She often managed to find a few hours of stolen pleasure in the arms of the lovers ousted by Eva. However, this one, she wanted for herself. She did not want to smell the perfume of her sister on him. She wanted him to see her win this beauty contest, but like every time, the star of the evening went to the brilliant Eva, who unequivocally wooed all those who approached her. Her smile like Mona Lisa, her hips, and her generous breasts were full of promise in her tight silk sheaths.

Luce felt like a substitute for Eva. When Eva broke up with her boyfriends, Luce was happy. But Benjie... Benjie was different. Her love was pure, but he never looked at her as anything other than the little sister who he must endure to please the eldest, despite the prompts and provocative attitudes she multiplied, going so far as to throw herself on him in the absence of Eva.

Here in Haiti, everyone knew this or that voodoo ritual, or the words that brought luck or love, repelled misfortune, cured some ills, or helped women in giving birth. Everybody avoided the *quat'chemins* when a rooster was seen bleeding, legs tied, deposited in the early morning or during the night. Better not to ask questions. It was necessary to remain silent; to close your eyes. However, the final rite was the witch, and her alone. She dialogued with the powerful *loas*, these hybrid divinities, a mixture of Christian beliefs and paganism.

One night, while Eva was at a party organized by the hairdressing professionals in their town, Luce slipped into their bed when Benjie had gone to bed early, exhausted by his work week. She gave herself shamelessly to him, in the darkness, clinging to him to share his desire. She woke him up under the blanket. For a few minutes, surprised, he had not pushed her away. He sighed and gently grasped her hair to bring her to him. She thought she was winning, but suddenly, he threw off the blanket. He discovered the deception and threw her out of bed. He spoke to her in nasty words. Eva was his lover and his wife, reproaching her and condemning her initiative to seduce him.

Her hate was born that night, and she swore revenge to do anything in her power to disunite this unbearable couple. He was magnanimous and swore to her that he would never do anything to hurt Eva; that he loved her sister and no one else. Fidelity was the most important thing in a couple. Luce then nourished the idea to make him swallow his disdain. She knew her sister well, and Eva was not of the same opinion. For her, men were consumables, but she did not want to leave Benjie, who represented in her eyes a kind of assurance of respectability, even if she flirted with the young boys that Luce often presented.

Despite the heat of the already fallen tropical night, Luce shuddered that she would have to return to Mama Calixte the following week. She was afraid. The witch's hooked fingers would no longer be satisfied with the three hundred dollars she slipped into her questionable claws. She would have to pay four times more, but she was determined to go all the way. The spells, the charms, and the remedies of witchcraft were pegged to the body of most Haitians, raised in families like hers, who took advantage of their uses, like the Africans, the Antilleans, the Brazilians. She knew she could no longer escape. Eva forgot their origins. She lived in New York since the age of six. But Luce came later to join the family in the United States. She spent all her childhood and part of her adolescence in the skirts of her paternal grandmother in the country. Old Petronella was among those who were suspicious of whites, and who preserved their culture and beliefs. The only sacrifice she made was the almost daily practice of the rites of the Baptist church, which she frequented assiduously, mingling the power of the Christian saints with the voodoo forces, to which she resorted to as much as was necessary.

The stories of the old women were still in her memory, and Mama Calixte populated the world of her childhood. She always loved to listen to the tales of people who exchanged recipes of love potions and concoctions with therapeutic virtues, grouped at the vigil, mumbling their secrets in

Creole, drawing on their clay pipes or their little black cigars.

If she were not immersed in this belief in the supernatural and the powers of the *loas*, she would never have come back to meet Mama Calixte and call on her services. The approach seemed insane, irrational, not to mention costly, but she made the decision, quite naturally, in front of the vanity of her enterprises, to attract the man she desired the most in the world, who she loved and hated all at once.

For the time being, she took the bus back to her cousin's house. Luce breathed, a little relieved. She became aware of the thirst and hunger she felt, the sweat that clung to her flowery Indian dress. Soon she would meet Eva at Newark Airport to return to New Jersey—another world—and she could weave the canvas of her dirty work.

Roxane, her cousin, prepared a dish of rice and peas with grilled chicken, flavored with spices. They ate in silence. Roxane knew the purpose of her cousin's outing that day, but made no comment on the contents of the brown bag that Luce had in a travel bag. While Roxane settled down in front of her small television to watch the rest of her evening soap opera, Luce showered for a long time, as if to wash herself from those hours spent in the old town, in the smoke of the blackish hut, and a vague feeling of guilt emerged. How would Eva react? Would she be too disappointed if her lover found himself in Luce's arms? She thought about Ingrid, her niece, who liked Benjie and considered him almost a substitute dad.

She went to bed at once, exhausted, but failed to find the restful sleep she counted on—the restless mind of a thousand contradictory thoughts. She wondered how she could discreetly bury the doll with hexes in the garden of the pretty house where Eva and Benjie planned to settle, at a precise hour, a dark moonlit night. Well, she would find it! This seemed easier to achieve than the approach she had just taken. First, Benjie's attachment to her sister would weaken, while Eva would continue to run to the arms of other men. Then, once the treachery was discovered, she would play the role of the loving sister-in-law, ready to do anything to make the man happy.

She took her revenge by attaching Benjie irrevocably to her sister, despite the adventures and young lovers that she never tired of cumulating. Their future remained secure because he was about to become a prominent professor and a renowned writer, a poet, and why not a diplomat, as he often said? Luce imagined herself alive in the golden wake of this couple, frequenting a brilliant and high-class environment, where no doubt she, too, would finally find the man she would marry. She would leave her obscure job as a temporary secretary to mingle with wealthy people, travel with her sister, and have a good time. This bastard would be madly in love with her sister, and finally humiliated, cuckolded in her own home, and she could without remorse, conquer him. She should not have been in such a hurry. She should have waited until he was more desperate, feeling betrayed and abandoned, and he could have taken refuge in her arms. She blamed herself for not being more patient. However, she would be avenged.

THE FOLLOWING WEEK

Mama Calixte, sitting on a stool, her hair caught in her cotton handkerchief, was puffing on a little cigar. Her opulent chest spread over her lap. She did not look at her visitor. She stared intently at a cauldron where a mixture was simmering on a tripod in front of her. Sometimes, it seemed like she whispered something between two puffs of her smelly cigar, her lips barely stirring. The smell of the broth invaded the dark room.

Luce thought she recognized the smell of fish and thyme, but something stronger prevailed behind the smell that might have passed for a simple fragrant fisherman's soup, as if a rotten egg had fallen there inadvertently. She scarcely dared to breathe, so as not to disturb the old woman's meditation, who beckoned her to take a seat on a chair in front of her without a word. The minutes stretched out for hours, and the heat began to bother the young woman who felt sweat halos wet the armholes of her cotton shirt.

Suddenly, the old woman stood up with surprising agility for her age and grabbed a jar on a shelf. She plunged her right hand in and grabbed something that she sprinkled around Luce. It looked like ashes. She put a pinch on each of her shoulders and her head. The young woman recoiled thinking that her white shirt would be stained.

"This will protect you," mumbled the witch finally, "You carry the evil spell with you, and you may see him turn against you, because you go beyond the oceans for him to be with you. Be careful not to touch him now without saying the words that I am going to tell you that will give you the veil of protection with these ashes. *"Akou', akou'desse to protect mwen, menaj or wa, nan noun serving 'Calixte, powetesse nan prop name li, kap bound and untied by the power of secrecy wou yo and magic'w yo."*

Luce suddenly felt cold temples, and her mind clouded. Then, Mama Calixte said to her, "I am going to give you a little of this drink, which you will have to absorb tonight at sunset for three days. You will do the same thing the day you bury the doll, and when you see that man for the first time when you are home."

Luce remained silent. She never told the witch that she came from the United States and that she had to go back there. Indeed, she went beyond the oceans.

"However," added the witch, "This man will suffer. You will succeed in disuniting them, but he will never be your lover because his heart is too pure, unless you know how to persuade him with patience and a lot of genuine love... or else, it will take a much stronger and much more expensive magic, and today I am tired."

Luce turned pale in the face of a half-success, and her hatred was all the greater. Anger overcame her, but she was too afraid of the spell caster to retort, so she tried not to let her disappointment show. She reached only part of her goal. She wanted the witch to think she was manipulated. But on the other hand, if Mama Calixte, whose powers were recognized by most Haitians, could not attach Benjie's heart to hers, it's because it was really impossible at the moment. But one day, maybe eventually. The important thing was to separate him from Eva.

The return to the city seemed even harder than the week before. A thousand thoughts agitated her, and she began to work out other plans. If she could not have Benjie, she was certain that Eva would not stay with him anyway, so she would perform the ritual to the end.

Luce was still young, so she ended up thinking about Dominique, the man she had been with for a while. Dominique was far from matching the ideal man she thought she detected in Benjie for herself. He was boring, harsh, loved the game, women, and drank a lot; but on a sexual level, she knew he was happy when he was not too drunk. He did not have the level of culture and knowledge of Benjie either. His world was of odd jobs: a plumber, a storekeeper, a deliveryman. He did not know how to make long-term plans.

The only thing she was sure of was that he felt certain feelings about her, and that she could bring him to the pageant without too much trouble. He would be flattered to be distinguished by the beauty of his lady. Luce knew she was a pretty girl, pleasant to look at and elegantly dressed. She liked to spend money on jewelry and accessories of all kinds, and until now, she always relied on her sister's money to satisfy her desires.

Benjie's earnings would assure them all this excess. This would be difficult to do with the inconstancy of Dominique and his famous habit of being more often unemployed than a salaried worker. The future seemed rather compromised and troubled for Luce. Eva with her hair studio could always get by. She had to get closer to Dominique and try to catch him. It was necessary to change some plans. It was also necessary to follow the evolution of the loves of her sister, and Benjie, who would suffer.

All these contradictory thoughts were jostling in disorder in Luce's head, which was very troubling and uncomfortable. To reassure herself, she thought of the cruise she was going to take with the family, since Benjie offered the tickets. Luce remembered during the rickety taxi ride back to the heights of the city.

MAMA CALIXTE

A slight smile passed the lips of Mama Calixte, who finished chewing her little cigar. She remained a few more minutes sitting on her stool without moving, her eyes distant after the young woman left her lair. She got up and walked to the dark background of her hut, then slid the wall of wood that served as a partition.

There, anyone who could have witnessed this scene would never have believed their eyes. It was a total and striking contrast to the poor hut supported by a mitten post, full of smoke from the boiling cauldron, cluttered with a quantity of *wanagas*, vases, pots, candles of all colors, and red, black, and white feathers to attract beneficial spirits. In the jars lined up on a rickety shelf were the dried carcasses of frogs, *zandolites*, and vipers. Two ceremonial drums hung from a nail.

The old witch closed the sliding partition into a charming little living room, all made of clear rattan and adorned with colored cotton. On the wall were framed portraits representing the Black Madonna of Guadalupe, who had all her devotion, and the Sacred Heart, with euphoric glances and rays of light prolonging their outstretched hands. On the other side was a coaster with cabalistic signs, painted red, on an ivory parchment. In a small library were fifteen carefully lined black moleskin notebooks, a large dictionary, a Bible, an atlas, and some books on the virtues of plants.

In front of the portrait of the Virgin burned a candle, and in front of the frame under glass on a pedestal table sat a perfume burner, a large rather baroque crystal inkwell with two penholders on a writing-desk, and two blocks of correspondence.

Mama Calixte, who had hardly ever been to school, knew how to write well enough, and only knew how to use the ancient penholder from her days at the elementary school. She was placed for three years in the religious institute, where she stayed as a child after the death of her parents, before being entrusted as a young teenager to a vague cousin of her mother. The relative was a voodoo priestess, who kept Calixte more as a young housekeeper, cook, and assistant. She raised her without particular tenderness, but with care, respect, and righteousness.

"You will succeed, and you will be respected," she repeated often. "People will fear you, and you will know all their secrets because they will come to find you, forgetting their arrogance and their social rank, to solicit your help. You will have to try to solve problems by being smarter than them... learn, my daughter, learn, because you have been chosen poor to serve, but you will be rich. Only be discreet about your fortune, and do not waste it."

The teenager often wondered how she could call herself rich when she lived in a dirty and smoky hut, and when she did not wear nice clothes or have a carriage like the people of the city.

She finally understood little by little when she realized that the food Mama Félicité served was good and plentiful. The meat and the fish never failed. The vegetables, the fruits, the fresh eggs, the chocolate, the milk, sugar, flour... everything was ready to consume. The food was tastier and more diverse than the orphanage. She had few clothes, but they were in good condition. She had in addition to her simple everyday clothes, a flowered Indian dress, a cotton camisole, a petticoat, a fancy dress for festive days, comfortable sandals, and a little white cotton hat, too.

She was intrigued by the travels that old Félicité sometimes undertook. She left town for about a week to take her medicine to the country and get the simple things she needed for her potions. At other times, she filled a small suitcase of the essentials, adjusted her gloves and hat, and put on a flowery dress and her patent shoes as if it were a Sunday or a holiday, and put Calixte in-charge of the shop. She told her to give this or that remedy to the people who would come in her absence, and Calixte scrupulously observed her recommendations.

She was not complaining, because she was curious about the witch's activities, and she read and reread Félicité's notebooks dealing with magic. She sometimes plunged into scripture reading because there was a Bible in Félicité's library. She listened to the radio and liked songs in Creole that spoke of love. She knew almost no boy of her age. She sorted medicinal plants, dried them, crushed those that served to make powders, and was satisfied with her modest condition.

However, she knew that other people suffered from hunger and misery, and that there was so much violence in her country. She heard about the state police, the *tontons macoutes*, the disappearances, the tortures, the torment of the inflamed tire as punishment for these murderers, and the torture of *PèLebrun*, but it seemed to belong to another world she did not know, or refused to know.

Her horizon was normally limited to the town of Pétion Ville, where she lived, and a few shopping streets downtown, where she sometimes went shopping for the house: thread, needles, a few meters of fabric, ink, and candles for rituals or power outages. The rest was bought from the many street vendors.

On those days, Calixte was allowed to stroll an hour or two on the boulevard Jean-Jacques Dessalines and enjoy a lemon sherbet—her only sin. The cars and the crowd made her dizzy, so she did not stay long and quickly went back to the suburbs, hailing a crowded taxi and ignoring the groups of young people who gave her strong glances or sometimes tried to address her. She bought books and newspapers: "The Morning," the "Novelist," the "Bon Nouvèl," or the "Boukan," that she flipped through during the trip, but that she would read the following days with great interest because she loved to read, and she learned so many things.

She did not have a friend her own age, except a companion of misfortune who she met at the orphanage and married at a very young age. She left to live in the country with her husband. She heard only rare news, except when Petronilla gave birth to another child or when her husband was very sick. Petronilla appealed to Mama Félicité, who did what was necessary to heal him.

Calixte also kept in touch with another girl she met at the Sunday service, Imelda, whose family was to leave for a distant journey. It seemed that there was a "country of cocaine" called "United States of America" where many citizens went because, it was said, life was better there than in Haiti. Sometimes Calixte wondered what this Promised Land looked like, trying to imagine cities bigger than her own, noisier streets with even more crowds, mountain views, lakes, factories... She felt happy to get back to Mama Félicité's little house, which was her haven and the only place she felt safe. In her heart, she was grateful. Mama Félicité sheltered her from all these things.

For Calixte's fifteenth birthday, Mama Félicité brought gifts back from her escapade of the week. She offered her a dictionary, an atlas, new clothes, and a gold chain with a medal of the Virgin of Guadalupe. Calixte wondered how Félicité was able to obtain these objects. It was her first real gift since the death of her parents, and her eyes filled with tears.

"Here, my daughter, I know that you like to read. It is time for you to know that we live in a very small country and that many bigger countries, huge lands beyond the ocean, surround us. There are people of all kinds who speak languages that you will never understand. However, you must know their existence because you will have to one day render those services, too."

Calixte felt great emotion, and thanked her benefactor with much affection. Sometimes it occurred to her that Félicité would not live forever and that she would end up alone all by herself again. However, she quickly chased away those ideas, wishing nothing more than to become a voodoo priestess and develop her powers for the service of others.

Calixte took care of the housework and stored the vials as she was taught. She had a little lodging next to the hut, three rooms with a small kitchen, and even a little cabinet, where she washed and got ready for Sunday service.

Old Félicité did not have a lot of furniture, apart from an imposing large bed that dated back to the colonial era. She had a small couch in the room that was allocated to Calixte, an antique wooden table surrounded by four chairs furnished with straw, and three heavy boxes, where she folded her work clothes and her beautiful Sunday clothes. She also owned a varnished straw hat, adorned with a little flowery bouquet, cotton gloves, a black lacquered bag, comfortable shoes that were old and rather worn, and moleskin-covered notebooks full of fine writing in violet ink. "All the secrets are there," she said, "They will be yours one day. I have no one to succeed me, except you."

Calixte was given a lower chest, which encumbered the floor of the little room, and a narrow table where she placed a kerosene lamp. At that time, she did not have much. The meager clothing that the nuns gave her, some yellowed pictures of her parents, and the framed photo of the Virgin of Guadalupe, which survived miraculously from the house where she lived with her family, were all her fortune. The crystal inkwell was her first personal purchase.

Félicité died one afternoon while taking a nap, while Calixte was preparing a potion in the hut. She, as a shy and now a doubly orphaned girl, called on the help of the neighbors to run for the doctor, who lived so far away, and take the steps for the funeral, forcing herself to look into the valuables of Mama Félicité, whose secrets she always respected. She then learned, thanks to the notary of Grandville, that the old witch bequeathed her all her possessions, which consisted not only of the little house, which constituted her outbuildings, but also of a house in the countryside toward the Anseaux-Galets. She then understood where the good eggs came from, the poultry, and the vegetables that Mama Félicité brought back from her secret travels.

In her legacy was a well-stocked savings booklet, apparently fueled by unexpected gains at La Borlette, and an opulent Lamartiniere house, with fine furniture and all modern comforts. So, the one who adopted Calixte went from time to time to rest in her small country house or to spend a few days in her beautiful apartment, where she received a particular clientele. Some were said to have come from abroad to consult the old witch, and paid her considerable fees to succeed in business, recover her health, and ward off a competitor. Even a movie star, whose fame was a little down and who wanted to regain a contract! Mama Félicité had a well-filled address book. The only condition was to continue in the path traced by Mama Félicité, to perpetuate her work and pass on her secrets, the famous notebooks, whose rituals should not be lost.

Calixte gladly accepted this saving legacy and pledged to dedicate her life to the service of others through the science of voodoo and magic. That's why she bought this beautiful inkwell, always full of moleskin notebooks, similar to those she copied when she completed her rituals. She had enough capital to furnish the apartment in town to her taste, which served as a workroom one week a month, and to modernize the house adjoining the hut. She bought a refrigerator and a supreme luxury: a small TV. Now, she discovered the world and could visualize everything she discovered in her reading.

She went on regular trips to the farmhouse to rest from time to time, butcher her prosperous poultry, or make a small trade with the brave mulatto who managed her property. She liked to grow herbs and pick them for her powders and potions. She accumulated revenue over a long time because her fame was established and satisfied her customers.

Mama Calixte, reciting her memories and gathering her ideas, lit white candles and knelt before her Virgin of Guadalupe. She gave a mischievous little smile at the thought of the ritual she just performed on the elegant young woman, who she knew. She recalled the letter sent by her old acquaintance who went to the United States. Imelda told her of her disappointment due to the inconstancy of her grandson, Dominique, who could not maintain himself or keep a job. He was also very much in love with a young girl.

Imelda was convinced that if this girl gave her grandson the love she was yearning for, he would do something to build a successful life. To the beat of her drums, Mama Calixte eagerly asked to meet this woman. It was served on a platter.

Admittedly, she would satisfy the request of the woman who came with an unruly heart for

277

revenge to destroy a union. Mama Calixte did not like to cause trouble, so she gave the spell limits and imagined a "happy end" that Luce would never imagine. She replaced hatred with love, even if she had to pay her own debts by activating the disunity of another couple. She knew that the victim, Benjie, would eventually be rewarded with happiness. The suffering would be temporary. She mentioned a well-known proverb: *Pa gen pèn san sekou*, which meant "there is no suffering without deliverance."

In the drink consumed by Luce, Mama Calixte ground hot pepper and the fertilized egg of a white hen, sacrificed to Erzulie, so that the union could be realized. She invoked the big *loas* of love for Dominique and Luce. She finished her devotions and crossed herself several times, then washed her face and hands in a small bowl of enamel, wiped herself with a white cloth, and returned to the hut, carefully closing the movable wall behind her. She then began chanting an incantation after seizing one of the tambourines that accompanied her chant. Her closed eyes accelerated the pace gradually until her body began to twitch, move, and turn on her, throwing her into a trance that left her exhausted, broken but satisfied to have accomplished what she had for The Conquerors.

(...) Every evening hoping for an epic tomorrow,
The phosphorescent azure of the Tropic Sea
Enchant their sleep with a golden mirage;

Where, bending over white caravels,
They watched as new stars ascended
To an unknown sky
From the depths of the ocean
Some new stars.

- José Maria de Heredia

Persuaded that the best way to tame my gazelle was to marry her, I decided with indescribable enthusiasm to fall, naively, into the error that cost me so much. The question should be asked in an unforgettable place, and be a moment of paradise. The cruise she dreamed about for so long would probably weigh a little heavy on my budget, but it was worth it.

The series of decisions I took then, seemed to me, to be the measure of my immoderate love; to ask for her hand; to offer her a ring certainly beyond my means, but symbolizing our idyllic union. We would embark on a cruise along the coast of the Atlantic and discover beautiful exotic countries whose evocative names danced in our ears: The Gulf of Mexico, Honduras, Belize... I would make myself a rich, handsome, and romantic Hollywood hero, completed by an African princess of ebony skin. All the ingredients of the movies of the fifties with a happy ending would be gathered, and the bridal march already resounded in my ears.

I rushed to the nearest travel agency and made the reservations in ten minutes for the Thursday of the following week. I occupied my morning by making some indispensable purchases for the occasion in New York. After a short lunch on the run, I walked the avenues in search of a rare stone to seal our engagement with dignity—something sparkly for my Eternal Eva. *They were going to conquer the fabulous metal.*

On a cloud, I walked through the door of the jewelry store, whose sober windows contrasted with the glare of the displays inside. A cozy atmosphere in the purest tradition. A well-dressed sales representative with a discreet smile saluted me ceremoniously. With a gesture of this arm, I was invited to discover, on these dark velvet restorations, diamonds of all sizes, extravagant rings, earrings, and necklaces. The shine fascinated me. I thought back to the expression "rivers of diamonds," and I admitted its accuracy. The thousand fires of their light flowed in real cascades.

Having so much magnificence, my heart was panicked, and my head felt like it was heating up. The seller started by asking what I wanted to buy, what kind of jewel, and for what occasion. I expressed myself in a brainless voice. Did he see my trouble? I could not explain what I wanted, so he gave his pitch. What is suitable? A diamond yes, a diamond. It is pure, it is chic, it is so symbolic, it is eternal. He described the original Baroque setting of this one, the exceptional size of this one, the artistic facets of this other. I did not know which one to choose. I did not even have the reflex to ask for the price of the jewels.

Suddenly, sitting on her immaculate silk cushion, I saw it, in a case as dark red as its extraordinary brilliance: the ruby. I could not interest myself in anything else. The ruby will be placed on the finger of my beautiful Eva. Daring to seize it, I probed its depth. It seemed infinite. Her blood red color shimmered and spoke to me in secret. She whispered, "Yes, I will marry you. Yes, I want you for life," and her whisper took the accent of my love.

The seller felt that the deal was done, even before I detached my eyes from this wonder. A diamond seemed to me too common for the occasion. "How much for the ruby, please?"
I felt like croaking and did not listen to the answer.

I left like a thief almost, the package tight against me. I ran to the subway, slipping it into the inside pocket of my coat and all the way to the parking lot where I left my car. I did not stop pressing her, as if I were to lose her. I did not even think of the four astronomical checks I gave the sales representative, shaking because I sensed his contempt when I offered to pay him over time. However, in five days, we will start on a new foot and enter, eager for passion, this marine intoxication that will cradle us before throwing us on the shores of a new happiness.

Back in my little apartment, I no longer delayed building a thousand plans for the future. First, I would have to move, then find a large and bright home where Eva and her daughter could have a room, and an office for myself, in a neighborhood near the school she attended.

I imagined new decorations. A haven for all those memories and kitsch and idiotic objects I piled up during my life with Ariane. Exit Ariane. I was cured. I liked distinguished colors: burgundy, gray, ivory, and black. This evocation made me want to laugh. I have never worried about these things! What was happening to me?

Like a snake, I left my molt, and found myself rejuvenated and revitalized. I thought about her, Eva, the woman of all my dreams. Eva, my saving grace, my soon-to-be wife. What beautiful days ahead: family Sunday's devoted to our hobbies, romantic walks, our favorite movies, rainy afternoons under the duvet. We intoxicated each other without restraint.

We would have children, our children. I dreamed of a beautiful and big family where Ingrid could play the big sister. Laughing, screaming, little feet running up the stairs where we would stumble on an abandoned toy. It was no longer an apartment, but a house we would need. A garden where we could barbecue with neighbors and friends and blow out birthday candles, more and more over the years. Eva would be the queen of this happy tribe, and we would sink in the evenings, exhausted but happy in the marriage bed to make love again.

How long exactly did this daydream last? I did not know. The night was almost gone, and I heard the familiar sounds of the floor above, the heels of the Madame, who finally took off her shoes. I heard the music that invaded the apartment regularly when the son, a clumsy but polite teenager, put his stereo up until his mother told him to lower the sound. Finally, I heard the heavier steps of the father, a municipal official that I practically never crossed.

It was the loud ringing of my landline that shook me and pulled me out of that bliss. I jumped to grab it, sure to hear the warm and modulated voice of my darling. It was her, who asked me if my day was good. I could not contain myself and revealed to her that I conceived the idea of finally leaving with her for ten days on the cruise I always talked about. I asked her to free herself professionally because we had to have this romantic getaway. I enthusiastically described the benefits that the agency told me that morning.

"My love, you are so cute!" She said. "I am sure it will be no problem for my job. I have many vacation days to take, and this will allow us to be together and relax. To sunbathe, to visit those countries that I want to see. Candlelit dinners, stopover shopping, chic evenings at night. I'm crazy excited, and I know that they will be, too. I will call them."

She was laughing on the other end of the line, but overcome by a shadow of anxiety, I suddenly pulled myself together and asked her, "Who...who?"

"Ben, darling, my sister and my mother. You know that my daughter goes to her father's house for two weeks, starting next Wednesday. We will be free."

I could not articulate a response right away without betraying myself. I did not want to believe it.

"You are not saying anything. Do not tell me you did not plan to take my sister there, at least? You know she is not doing well right now since the breakup with Marc, and you think that my mother should be left all alone? I am not being selfish. You just do not understand..."

Blah-blah-blah and blah-blah-blah. No! I did not think. Yes! I wanted to be selfish, *me*. Yes! I wanted to be alone with her and leave behind the mother and sister, her eternal counsels. Her sister, with her stories of incessant breakups and untimely encounters, left her in an almost continuous state of depression and always on the verge of tears.

I had not considered things in this light, anyway. Farewell dreams of idyllic love, one-on-one, languorous, intimate evenings leaning on the railing. "We look up into a sky unknown from the bottom of the ocean new stars," Jose Maria de Heredia had said so well.

However, you have to fight against bad luck with good heart. Quite confused, I evaluated on the one hand, and at full speed, the disappointment of not undertaking this cruise with my beautiful Eva. I was concerned my marriage proposal and this first honeymoon might take place between two agitated episodes of our life, resembling more than a period of showers and clearings between storms. On the other hand, I thought about the cost of the trip, knowing the expensive propensities of the mother and daughter, not to mention the tickets they would probably never intend to pay for. I tried unsuccessfully to make a rough calculation of the first expenses—two tickets for the cruise. I hoped that they would share at least the same cabin and would not require to each have their own, especially with my sister-in-law, who no doubt would be looking for a love affair once again. I was not convinced at all. Tomorrow, I needed to return to the agency again to settle this matter, hoping that there would be tickets available. Ah, Monsieur de la Fontaine, you were right: "Farewell, calf, cow, pig..." It took so little to ruin everything.

I heard Eva get impatient. "Well, you are not saying anything. What is it?" Her tone changed and took on that acidity that I knew by heart, that blame and anger, of which our relationship already suffered to the point of separating.

I sighed, "No, it is nothing. I was thinking because I have to go back to the agency to confirm. Are you sure they will come? I was wondering if... they were available, too."

Why take refuge in the lie? Because I was eager to love and to be loved, to save that wobbly relationship that I could not, and did not, wish to extricate myself from — that I dedicated my life to from that moment on. Because I wanted to believe in it, and commit myself to the love that failed me and missed me. Because I planned everything, and that splendid ruby that I had just acquired, so dear, was waiting to be worn by the one who I wanted to be my wife. Me, the poet with a broken heart, did not want to know the pangs of loneliness, jealousy, lack of another. I needed Eva's daily life, her caresses, her laughter, her quirks, and her bewitching body. I belonged to her body, and I could not imagine that she did not feel mine, too.

She continued for a few minutes talking about other things and did not even think of thanking me for the gift I just gave her family. We parted on a "Goodnight, my love, we will call tomorrow!" Which left me with a bitter aftertaste.

I begin to know disappointment like the back of my hand, since this was the umpteenth woman who upset my world and made me desperate! However, today, Wednesday, the day before our departure for our romantic—now family—getaway, what fell on my head was not without interest in the field of great "disillusions."

My love woke me at dawn with a phone call complaining about and recriminating her ex-husband, Ingrid's father. I waited for the floods of anger to calm before I tried to understand what was happening. She yelled insults in my ear. I did not like when she got in these states because her vulgarity bothered me.

"Calm down, my beauty, what is going on?" It was hard for me to interrupt her.

Her ex decided he could not take their daughter this week because he had an important match. (By the way, what sport does he play? Oh yes, basketball!) I did not immediately understand the seriousness of this announcement, so I started to reassure her that Ingrid would see her father another time.

Then, the consequence of this situation hit me. This meant that we would have to take the teenager with us on the cruise, because the only people who could take care of her were her grandmother and her dear aunt. No! No! No, it was not possible. There was no more room on this boat, and everything was finalized.

The other two would never give up the tickets I had so much trouble finding. We were not on the same bridge of the ship, which had already upset the ladies. What to do? I could not cancel. I would not be reimbursed. Are there kennels for teenagers when their parents go on vacation?

I could not say anything because my thoughts did not come to order. I did not even answer Eva's calls, who was screaming on the phone, "Hello! Hello! Benjie, where are you, damn it? You listen to me! What are you doing?"

I did not like that harpy voice she used to talk to me, but I had to save the situation and reassure her that I was the man she could count on in all circumstances. Her future husband. At this evocation, my heart squeezed. I could not believe that we would begin the dawn of our next life together this way.

"Do not worry, darling, it is really not a problem. I will phone the agency when they open. Ingrid will come with us. I think she will enjoy this trip. I will call you back, I love you!"

Why was that last phrase suddenly fogged in my head? I had the impression that it cracked as soon as I pronounced it.

"OK, Benjie, I love you, too. We will see each other tonight, do not forget! I will do things you like, darling, you know!"

My coffee spilled while I was shaving, and of course, I cut myself. I tapped the blood with a Kleenex. "Shit!" I rarely used curse words because I liked to have more polite language. I lowered my head to seize the Kleenex that fell to the ground, and stained my white shirt with blood. No, bad luck was chasing me! I had only one shirt left. The others were already in my travel bag. I fell back on a faded polo because the newer one was also stored in the bag. I thought about what would happen if I could not find room for Ingrid. I should also call my banker to ask for a credit check because the state of my finances was beginning to worry me. I had not considered all these hazards.

Tired of wearing their haughty miseries De Palos, de Moguer, truckers and captains, Leaving drunk with a heroic and brutal dream.

I believed that dreams of passion flew away, caught up in human reality, inconstancy, and vanity. I wanted to dazzle the one I loved. Could she not love me for who I was? Could she not give me the privilege of her exclusive presence for a few days? I was tired of sharing and living through others' episodic presence. These moments that I wanted for us were again scattered and fragmented.

Enchant their sleep with a golden mirage
What sleep? What mirage is this? I no longer sleep,
I no longer dream, and the dark mirages on the horizon
disturb me without enchanting me.
Like a flight of giants out of the mass grave
Their shadows hover over me.

LUCE

Luce watched Mama Calixte attentively, but with some fear. She lit a black candle and finished sewing the doll that was to enslave her enemy and cause her sister to maintain a passion for this man.

"I transfer your essence into the body of this doll. By the power of similarity, you are one with her. Your name is now known by demons. I have you in my power as long as I want."

Mama Calixte piqued her heart and head several times. The doll was supposed to represent the one Luce hated with all her strength. Had she not rejected it under the pretext of fidelity?

"... Because I decided that way." The old woman blew three times on the red rag doll and waved bells, that she grabbed off a shelf, three times. She still chanted a few sentences in a language that Luce did not understand and seemed to remain motionless for a few minutes.

"There, my fair lady, the *loas* have heard us." She took a little black cigar from the back of her pocket and began to chew it, as if still lost in inaccessible thoughts.

Luce felt a cold air pass through her back and an intangible fear made her shudder. Sitting cross-legged on a colored mat, she felt dizzy, but scolded herself. What she came for was worth being frightened and paying for the service. It was no longer possible to go back.

Mama Calixte handed her the doll wrapped in a canvas bag and grasped with her hooked fingers the brown envelope containing the price of the ritual. Then she blew on the black candle and scattered in a bowl the ashes of coal that had been used to burn the incense at the beginning of the ceremony. Luce did not know if she had to get up, but Mama Calixte, with a gesture of the hand, made her understand not to move. Finally, the old witch took the fine ashes between her fingers and let them slide back into the bowl. These formed then a kind of ring, then a second ring, which seemed to be inserted in the first, a little clearer than the first one.

"Woman.... You will soon find a husband, my dear!" The old woman was still absorbed in her thoughts and her eyes fixed on the ashes. She repeated, "Yes, a loving husband, but take care not to weary him. I do not tolerate frivolous and capricious women for long."

Luce remained perplexed. She did not come for this purpose, but this revelation rejoiced her. "A husband, when? I did not come for that. I came for a connection, but not for me."

"The *loas* spoke, my daughter, do not challenge them. They do what they want eventually. I say what I saw!"

The old woman got up pretty well for her age. But, how old could she be? Luce felt incapable of giving her an age: fifty, sixty, seventy. She looked young at times. Her eyes sparkled, and there were no wrinkles on her face, but she seemed so deep and so full of knowledge that she could have been alive for decades. The skin of her hands was parched, and the locks that escaped from her white cotton cap were of a steel gray.

THE CRUISE

Sun of my joy, Angel Cute
Descends, comes to reopen with your fingers the star
Of my heart Of your fingers go up
All the sunken ships of my childhood
Take me where the transparent conches swim
Among the seaweeds
And roll me of pleasure.
I am yours
Midi blue
At the top of its stem
Angel Cute. Sun of my joy
Come down pick, me (...)

I love you, and do you understand
These words? Answer.
The butterfly says them to the roses
The bud says them to the flower
Do you hear me say them?

- *Life Heart*, Xavier Orville

The trip by plane to Miami was drama-free. Eva sat next to me, and I held her hand in mine, looking out the window, happy just to have her close to me. In succession, on the row to our right, were her daughter, her sister, and her mother, chattering at length.

It was difficult to start any conversation with Ingrid, whatsoever. I sometimes observed her profile and loved her laugh. She looked happy and enthusiastic like a child. Her joy made me happy. I found her adorable as a whole in lavender silk, which emphasized her complexion of mulatto. As always, she was perfectly made up, a blue make-up softened her eyelids, and her hair gathered in auburn curls. I found her look classy and felt proud to see this woman at my side.

The sartorial purchases for this cruise were substantial, but I did not want to think of such down-to-earth problems. I brought some books for moments of relaxation. I wanted to discover French Creole literature from the West Indies and the African continent. I chose to read "The Mandate of Sembène Ousman," "The Beautiful Creole," by Maryse Condé, and a book by Xavier Orville, a Martinican writer who I hoped would not cause nostalgia for my last love, Marie-Reine, her compatriot.

My eyes fell on my companion, and I squeezed her cool hand, a prey to great emotion. This trip must be exceptional because I decided to take the plunge for the second and last time in my life to receive her as my wife forever. Yet, my happiness was at times darkened by the mourning I had just suffered. A great pain choked me when I mentioned the recent disappearance of my mother. I recited these verses taken from the novel "Heart, Life," and thought that it was beautiful and reassuring:

I missed her.
I would have liked her to share my amorous joy
And speak to me very softly,
As when I felt my first heartache,
As when I left my country to follow another destiny,
As when I returned from the school and we were waiting
for my father's return,
Sitting in the kitchen,

With that spice chicken stock,
Or fish fritters still floating in the air,
While dinner was simmering on the white gas stove.

I tried to regain courage. Mother dear, I thought, you who gave so much for your children, protect me from above, and do not be angry with me. My life is so full of love to give, and you left so much emptiness. I would like to realize that is why you made so many sacrifices. I closed my eyes, flooded with tears at the only memory of my mother.

The boat waiting for us made a great impression. Eleven floors of superimposed bridges, a real floating city where we were welcomed like kings in incredible luxury. The captain and his mate greeted their guests at the passage. The ship's staff, immaculately dressed, the fresh flowers arranged in the cabins, the corridors covered with soft carpets, and the welcome cocktail, should have plunged me into a sweet euphoria. However, alas, the annoyances started.

We booked two spacious cabins facing each other. One was for two people, and the other had three spaces. I was bitterly surprised to hear Eva say, "Here is your cabin," pointing to the double cabin for her sister and her mother. "Ingrid will sleep with us."

I could not believe it. I did not even have the opportunity to protest. She wanted her daughter close to her. Her decision was final, and she had the luggage arranged depending on that.

Luce and Ada rushed into their room to look for an elegant hat to watch the boat depart from the upper deck. The moorings dropped to the sounds of applause from spectators. The siren sounded three times, and "The Carnival Two" slowly started to make its way to the dream destinations that began to have a nightmarish flavor.

We unpacked our bags. The pool and spas were waiting for us. "Honey, let's go to the solarium." She donned a two-piece cheetah print bikini that made her more desirable and feline than ever. Grabbing her sunglasses, one of the flowered cover-ups bought for the occasion, her bath towel, and her golden sandals, we went out, flanked by her daughter. "Wait for me, I am coming too!"

"We will not wait for hours. We want to enjoy the pool before lunch," I said, my hand on the cabin door. However, I was giddy with ideas and scolded myself. *Why are you still so pessimistic? They are there to have a good time, too!*

I was ready in two minutes, but I quickly realized that I did not know exactly where to find them in this floating city. There were several solariums, several pools, and I spent nearly three quarters of an hour looking for them. Then, throwing myself into the first free deck I saw, I began to mull over my bad mood. I did not feel like reading the book I brought and decided to stay alone until lunchtime. I returned to the cabin to dress lightly. I was not hungry. I had to wait for their return for a while.

They came back laughing and chatting. I knew they were all three together. She did not notice my absence in the morning. She put on a white cotton dress, freshened up, and we went off with the family for lunch. There were more than ten restaurants on this boat, so the choice was difficult. We chose a Japanese restaurant to enjoy sushi and marinated fish with lime. The quality of the meal reconciled me a little.

Ingrid wanted to see a movie in the afternoon before going shopping with her mother and aunt. They spotted the shopping areas that promised them a good time. I found this idea great, convinced that we could take a nap and that I would have this afternoon for moments of intimacy that would be prohibited during the night because of the presence of the girl.

"Give me peace. I'm tired, I swam, I sunbathed, I am on vacation, I have to rest..." I did not know how many arguments Eva was able to oppose during this time when I tried to caress her, to share my desire with her, until she got up from the bed, apparently angry. Then, Luce knocked on the door to invite her sister to go on a walk and shop.

Feeling sick, I went on an adventure, walking through corridors, crossing couples hand-in-hand, young women in baiting suits, old women done up and covered with jewelry that shone on the wrinkled skin of their arms and necks. I ended up in one of the bars on the fifth floor. A piano played quietly, and I drank two martinis right after the other. Me, who never drank.

A beautiful woman gave me languid glances, and I looked at her in turn, but I suddenly got up, cursing the women and saying to myself, *One more that is not worth more than the others.* I felt disgusted with myself because I could have succumbed to this indirect invitation. Compared to Eva, all those women were so easy in appearance and so perverse in the end. However, I knew that my love was sincere, which made me think that I had to rush the marriage proposal to try to change her mood.

MOURNING

I loved the milky light that fell from the moon, the celestial dome where the stars blinked, and the lascivious palms asleep. The night was silent. No rustle disturbed the tropical tranquility. Yet, a few meters below, if I listened, I recognized the lapping sound of steady waves licking the shore. Only my pounding heart reminded me of my torment.

I began my nocturnal walk on the beach, systematically, despite the blood that hammered my temples, growing uncomfortable, as to delay the time to get there and face the reality of events. Roads followed each other gently. I met a few stray dogs, prowling in search of food. Up there, dogs were groomed and dressed like fairy monkeys, wearing ribbons or barrettes. Some were in the arms of their scented mistresses, others noble and arrogant being led on a leash in sanitized parks, along large avenues, or in cities sparkling with pride. These people treated their animals better than how children were treated in other countries. Ferocious meows rose from an upturned bin. A heap of starving cats, also driven by their misery. I heard snarling squeaks of rats defending their food against their own predators.

A few modest houses of indefinable color, surrounded by meager little gardens, sheltered numerous families of miserable fishermen. The yellow lights of the oil or gas lamps, or candles of fortune or misfortune, I said to myself, were extinguished, slowly plunging people into the dark to sleep, protect their children, and forget their daily ills, hunger, dirt, beatings, and hard work. Furtive and sweaty embraces in a corner of the adult hut were desperate acts of regeneration. Life, suffering, death, and love, through illusory enjoyment.

I envied the apathy of forgetfulness that would put them away from worry, despite their stomachs never satisfied, the anguish of tomorrow, the violence that tore them apart on a daily basis, and the slump in which my country was sinking. What unjust fate for them! Oh, precious moments of non-memory, waiting for a morning that would bring them back to despair too soon.

Up there in the clean city, the dinner served on white tablecloths dragged on, and discussions were probably fading in the bluish smoke of fragrant cigars. Beautiful white and flowery houses, behind their high walls in the warm night, still resonated with music and chatter about politics or the faltering economy of the country. To lament, certainly, but they were unaffected by it.

"By the way, Beatriz will marry the senator's son on Saturday. We are having a party before Antoine leaves for Harvard, do not let us down!"

The Duponsard family returned, delighted with their stay in Megève. "We will be in Paris, dear, in December. Nicole wants to renew her wardrobe."

"Which hotel will you stay at?"

I knew these two parallel and indifferent worlds, traveling the same roads with opposite destinies. Without resistance for the first, without remorse or conscience for the second, under the same heavens. In addition, what was I doing, only soul awake, deliberately refusing the refuge of forgetfulness, consumed in this ceaseless step toward the past, knowingly leading myself to face my memories? They walked beside me, like wolves on the lookout, never losing sight of their prey with their eyes. Still, hours of insomnia unrolled the long parchment of the past.

I imagined, stretched out in her little coffin of oak wood, a luxury that I gave her as the last bed of rest, my holy mother, Marguerite. My mother, with a heart of gold, whose breath was suspended "always and forever."

ABOUT THE AUTHOR

Lociano Benjamin earns a bachelor's degree in French from Montclair State University, in New Jersey. While at Montclair State University, he studied abroad at Sorbonne University/Nanterre University where he earned a License in Foreign Languages. Monsieur Benjamin has a master's degree in Diplomacy and International Relations from Westminster University/ Diplomatic Academy of London.

Former Adjunct Professor at the French Department of Montclair State University, Lociano Benjamin is a French Teacher at Abraham Clark High

School in Roselle, CEO of Radiodiplomacy2day in New Jersey. He is the author of Tears of Love (2002), 500 years of Exploitation, a Study of Diplomacy and Economics in Haiti (2010), French version (2015) by GEBCA edition.

The author he is an award-winning writer who was awarded a bronze medal in poetry from the French Academy of Paris in 1998, and the First Prize of a poetry contest from the French Consulate in New York for his poetry work in 2000 among other awards.

Lociano Benjamin has been living in the United States for over 30 years since his arrival in New York City form his motherland Haiti in the 80s. His dreams of professional success have been achieved greatly despite the odds and the numerous challenges he encountered in his journey in America.

Made in the USA
Middletown, DE
10 September 2021